Time
of
Castles

A SEARCH FOR ANCESTORS

L EIGH C LARKE

Order this book online at www.trafford.com
or email orders@trafford.com

Most Trafford titles are also available at major online book retailers.

Previous books: Land Above, Season's Sun, This and That, Now and Then and Puzzle of Suspects

Printed in the United States of America.

ISBN: 978-1-4669-9781-3 (sc)
ISBN: 978-1-4669-9783-7 (hc)
ISBN: 978-1-4669-9782-0 (e)

Library of Congress Control Number: 2013910213

Trafford rev. 07/10/2013

 www.trafford.com

North America & international
toll-free: 1 888 232 4444 (USA & Canada)
fax: 812 355 4082

In Memory of my Mother and Father

Chapter One

My mother spent her later years working on the genealogy of her family and seemed so excited when the timeline got back to early English, Welsh and Scottish nobles, their lives, their castles and the many names of important families of history she thought of as her great grandparents. In many cases these Anglo-Saxons led back to William the Conqueror (her favorite grandfather) and thus to France to Charlemagne, Germany to many Dukes and Italy where she located Mark Anthony as grandfather and Caesar as her uncle. One line, she said, even went as far back as the Egyptian Empire and found Nefertiti as her grandmother and several pharaohs as grandfathers. We all indulged her pastime and perhaps obsession, but it filled many hours and seemed to make her happy. I wondered if her primary family had left a void to be filled with all these historical people of her far past.

Her passion became my interest in an education that expanded into a PhD in History, with an emphasis on the medieval history of Great Britain. For five years I've looked into the faces of bright students taking my class as a requirement for their history major and I do my best to keep them interested. I am still filled with excitement each semester, not only in what I teach, but about the connections I make with the students in showing the importance of our past as it relates to our future. The men and women, great and lesser heroes, in past civilizations are our heritage and their timeline in history will become our own timeline for those that follow.

Sitting in our bright morning room over coffee and the Sunday morning paper, I looked at my serious faced husband, James, with his well-trimmed straight dark brown hair, his aristocratic Roman nose always topped with round glasses. What I loved most about him was his constancy; he was always the matter of fact, reliable man in my life. After a father whose journalistic career left his wife and child without his presence for most of the year, James fulfilled my need for dependability.

As he took a sip of coffee, I quickly attempted to get his attention, and for what seemed the sixteenth time that week, I said,

"Please James forgive me for seeming to be obsessive about this."

"But you are obsessive."

"You seem to think so, but I've this overwhelming feeling the time is now."

"If you must, then make your plans."

"But I want you to go with me."

"No, Leah; I can't take time away."

"Then I'll make plans to spend the next year in Great Britain. I wish we could do it together."

"I know, but it's your passion. Maybe you can join a travel group and I can come over for a couple weeks next summer."

"I don't like groups. I want to take my time, stop when I want, linger when necessary. I'll plan on leaving early next week. My sabbatical will allow me to stay long enough to finish my book and I'll look forward to you joining me when you can."

Later that week, as I packed my bags as lightly as possible, knowing I could buy necessities along the way, I felt uneasy about going without my husband, who in all things steadies my tendency to follow my father's genes in exploring the world. But perhaps time alone, after ten years on the straight and narrow with my perfectionist mate would allow me to indulge deep seated inquiries and to connect in some way with my ancestors who Mother loved to include as family. Along with my ancestral pursuits, I planned on collecting material for a book on the construction of early castles, which I needed to keep abreast of PhD publishing requirements at the university.

In the hours my United flight flew across timelines to London, I read all the notes I'd written for my itinerary with the help of my priceless guide book and used my Smart Phone to confirm my reservation at the Cavendish, London. I'd been in London a few times over the years, but wanted to return to Westminster Abby to check on the famous historical figures buried or commemorated there. I would stay two nights refreshing myself from jet lag, walk around Piccadilly Square and dine at some restaurants on my wish list.

From London I would rent a car, hopefully able to navigate on the wrong side of the road (wrong side to me). About five years earlier James and I did a driving tour to the countryside west of London and stayed for a time in Oxford, where James had attended years earlier. He drove most of the trip, but I did get in some practice, which would come in handy now as I planned on driving much further; from London to Land's End at Cornwall, where I wanted to see Castle Tintagel specifically and then into Wales, where my paternal grandmother's ancestors had lived, and especially the last true Prince of Wales. After visiting sites in England, I would arrive in Scotland where I wanted to research King James I and II and King Robert the Bruce, among others.

I planned to be frugal, but after not sleeping more than a couple hours at most on the plane, I felt pleased I'd decided to indulge somewhat in London and stay as close as possible to Trafalgar Square. I had stayed at the Cavendish on an earlier trip and it felt good to return; I remembered how comfortable the bed was and I couldn't wait to crawl into its luxury, although I would miss my special bed partner. I slept for six hours and awoke refreshed and ready for a day in London. The weather seemed cool for April, hazy, but no rain, as yet; I took my raincoat and umbrella just in case.

After breakfast at the hotel it was about twelve long blocks to the Abbey; a nice brisk walk to start the day. On an earlier trip to London I had taken the all day tour, including tea at Harrods, so this was just an opportunity for me to take more time at Westminster to think about the greats who are immortalized there.

In the early 600's a bishop by the name of Millitus had visions of St. Peter on this spot and he began building the Church of St. Peters at Westminster. King Edward the Confessor began rebuilding in 1042 and he and his wife were buried here before its completion in 1090. It was the first church in England built in the Norman Romanesque style. Although King Harold II is thought to have been crowned here, the first documented coronation was that of William the Conqueror, my 24th great grandfather.

Later, the first king to be buried at the Abbey, after King Edward, was King Henry VIII who had rebuilt the church in the Anglo-French Gothic style. Further rebuilding and restoration has taken place over the years. Many of the Plantagenet line of nobles have been buried here, and I will search out each of them in my travels, as many appear in my mother's genealogical studies.

As I reached this monumental structure, I stood in awe looking at its western façade and realizing the history contained within. I would pay respects to my great grandfathers and grandmothers and many other great notables buried or honored here; such as Darwin, Shakespeare and Churchill.

Wandering back towards my hotel I saw a grill I had read about and stopped for lunch. I'd had the hotel's complimentary English breakfast of scones and coffee and now I felt hunger pangs. Gordon Ramsey's Savoy Grill is well known for lunch menu affordability for such as me. I enjoyed a grilled steak hash with Burford brown eggs and chips, accompanied by a glass of English sparkling wine, which is getting good reviews.

Feeling contentment from my visit to Westminster Abbey and a great lunch I headed back to the hotel for a nice long nap.

Chapter Two

After another brisk walk about, strolling by the Tower of London and imagining the wives of Henry VIII being beheaded (thank God my mother did not locate him as a direct line ancestor), and remembering the site of the original London Bridge, now located in Lake Havasu City, Arizona, where James and I visited on one of our summer driving tours, I returned to the hotel to rest and then dress for 8 o'clock dinner reservations at the lovely Petrichor, Cavendish, London's own fine restaurant.

The restaurant looked absolutely fit for a king all dressed in fine linens, long velvet drapes and sculpted, golden walls. I glanced quickly to realize I was the only single in the room, but time had allowed me not to think 'single'; just one for dinner please. Single tables usually are located in way off corners, or close to where the waiters pass by from the kitchen, but the starched maître de escorted me to a small table at the edge of long bank of windows, where I could see the sparkling night lights. I would give him a big tip for his generosity. I enjoyed a duck salad with a delicious plum dressing and the Dorset Scallops accompanied by a glass of Italian Prosecco, champagne's sexy cousin. After dinner I stopped at the hotel lobby bar, where I ordered another Prosecco and asked the handsome bartender what he thought about driving to Cornwall.

"Are you experienced in driving our narrow country roads, closely surrounded by hedgerows?"

"No not really."

"It is a brutal drive to the south, if I were you I'd think about a motor coach."

"What do you think about the two day tour the hotel advertises for a coach to Penzance, with stops at many sites along the way?"

"Even for people who don't necessarily like tours, this one could be an exception. I hear people say they enjoyed it very much."

Handsome bartender got busy and I finished my drink, went to the travel desk and signed on to the tour beginning in the morning. Maybe I wouldn't be so brave in driving across Great Britain as I thought.

I called James around eleven when we decided it would be the best time to reach him.

"Hi honey." And I preceded to tell him about my trip so far and how I planned on taking a motor coach tour the next day.

"I thought you hated tours."

"This two day trip to Land End will be one of a kind; from there to Wales and onward I'll attempt to get local transportation, maybe trains or local buses."

"Sounds like catch-as-catch-can. Be careful Leah."

We said our goodbyes and I felt guilt over being away from him, just like my father, I thought. I tried to put all negative feeling from my mind and concentrate on the trip in the morning.

I awoke late and had to rush to grab a cup of coffee and toast with marmalade before I located the motor coach and found a window seat, all soft and reclining. The coach was very first class and I felt I had made a good choice. I wouldn't be able to view the countryside as well if I had driven. The passengers were all chatting, laughing and excited to begin. When the driver, smartly dressed in a uniform of white shirt with navy pants, appeared everyone quieted down and he introduced himself and then introduced his perky lady attendant, also attired in similar uniform, and said she would take care of all our needs.

Out first stop was at Runnymede where we drove through Windsor State Park amongst the many prancing deer in the green woodlands and where around the bend came in view the majestic Windsor Castle; a medieval castle and royal residence in the County of Berkshire. It was originally built for William the Conqueror after the Norman Conquest in 1066 and is the longest occupied palace in Europe. Later King John and then his son, Henry III, (both great grandfathers) built a luxurious royal palace inside the castle and he and later Elizabeth I made increasing use of the palace as a royal court and center for diplomatic entertainment. Later Queen Victoria made some changes to the palace and as the royal family today, used Windsor Castle for diplomatic entertainment and at present it is the weekend home of the Queen. The royal family lived here during the bombing of London during World War II and a fire in 1992 created damage that has been restored.

The site sits on around thirteen acres next to the River Thames, and the castle has features of a fortification, a palace and a small town. Although we only viewed it from the long walk, it is a sight of beauty I will long remember. In my notes I will use for by book on castles, I've included many facts about castles, their types, and histories, I will not cover here. But there's no doubt when you see Windsor Castle, you have seen the best of them.

Our next stop was in the village of Salisbury where we had a leisurely lunch at the Haunch of Venison, where we could glimpse the village reminiscent of medieval times and one of the best known markets in England. I was beginning to enjoy a couple who seemed to 'take me in' and had studied castles and inspired my lust for information. Later we stopped to view Salisbury's magnificent Cathedral with a 404 ft. spire, the highest in Europe, located on River Avon and then drove to Stonehenge to see the ancient and mysterious stone monoliths.

Amy asked, "Did your mother find these builders among your ancient ancestors?"

With a laugh, I said, "No, I'm afraid, she, as others, can't find any evidence or knowledge of these peoples."

That night we arrived in Bideford, above the river Torridge. The hotel Durrant House had a nice single room for me, and we enjoyed a welcome drink and dinner with our trusty tour director and fellow travelling companions. That evening Tom, Amy and I walked around the ancient seaport and visited about the many castles I would encounter on my search of ancestors.

After breakfast the next morning we travelled to the village of Clovelly and Dartmoor Heather, where we had a magnificent view of the moorland covered in heather. I wanted to set up an easel and paint. What a lovely view of purples and greens of all shades and some real sweet donkeys we got to pet. We then drove alongside the seaside resort of Boscastle along the coast of north Cornwall, where a fortress built in the 12th century barely survives, but draws tourists to view its beautiful seaport. We then headed back into Devon for a Devonshire cream tea and then to the ruins of Castle Tintagel, the reason for my adventure south.

An early fortification, built on a peninsula on Tintagel Island, later became Tintagel Castle built by Richard, Earl of Cornwall, in 1225, to establish trust from the Cornwall peoples who didn't like strangers in their domain. He built it to look more ancient than it was to reflect early legends depicting the location of King Arthur and the Knights of the Roundtable. I had always loved the stories of King Arthur; especially regarding Sir Lancelot and Guinevere, and my imagination had a field day. There is now some evidence to believe it could have been an early Roman settlement and later inhabited by Dumnonian Royalty in 4th to 8th century sub-Roman Briton.

We crossed an old footbridge to the Island and to the haunting ruins of the ancient castle and the panoramic view of the rugged Cornwall's seacoast and brilliant blue Atlantic Ocean. I closed my eyes and temporarily felt transported back in time, even though I knew of no ancestors that had inhabited Tintagel.

At the historic naval port of Plymouth, I did feel the presence of a much later ancestor. We came to the Mayflower steps at the historic naval port of Plymouth from which the Pilgrim Fathers set sail to America. Yes, one of my great grandfathers was on that first trip of the Mayflower to the new land.

Amy said, "When I get home, I'm going to set out to trace my genealogy."

"My mother became caught up in it and passed it on to me. I often dream as though I'm living in ancient times and sometimes it gets scary, rather mind bending."

"You seem quite sane to me."

"Well most of the time." And I laughed. "I'm thinking of jumping ship and going on to Wales from here. I've got so many places to visit; I must move on although I've enjoyed your company and know there are more interesting sites to see on this tour."

"We'll miss you and maybe see you later at some castle or another."

That evening we stayed at the Future Inn in Plymouth. Tom and Amy and I enjoyed too much wine with dinner as we shared stories and enjoyed each other's company. Back in my room, I called James to tell him of my plans, crawled into bed and soon found myself dreaming of King Arthur and his Knights of the Round Table. The wizard Merlin appeared before me (now being Guinevere, the king's wife), and said I must not ride off with Lancelot. Both Lancelot and I loved our King, but also loved each other. What could we do?

I woke up.

Chapter Three

S till feeling as if in a fog, I dressed and went down to have some coffee and scones and headed to the bus depot. My travel guide book said I could catch a bus to Cardiff, Wales and the 150 miles would take around two and half hours. I caught a first class bus, not as fancy as the tour bus, but comfortable seats and a big window to view the rolling lands, farms, villages, narrow hedgerow country roads and fast highways with gas efficient small cars you see all over Europe and Great Britain. I had a seat on the left side, so I caught a view of Dartmoor National Park with its tors, large rounded mounds with granite outcrops, looking strangely ethereal in the distance. Historical remains here date back to the Neolithic and early Bronze Age. Around these moors lies many mythic legends of headless horsemen, a bad large black dog, and pixies; even home of the Devil. I preferred the reality of the darling little Dartmoor ponies that live here.

Arriving in Cardiff, I grabbed my one check-on bag, adjusted my backpack and headed off to find my hotel. I'd made reservations at Park Plaza Cardiff in walking distance to the Cardiff Castle. I checked in and had lunch at the Neville pub, another name familiar in my genealogy, and ordered sausage toad in a hole and a pint. Nicely filled with unhealthy food and association with ghosts, I headed off to the castle.

The castle had been transformed from a Norman keep to a medieval castle and then a Victorian gothic mansion. William the Conqueror's oldest son Robert of Normandy, who attempted to take England from Henry I, a younger brother (ancestors) was imprisoned here until his death in 1134. Many of the nobles noted here in medieval times have ties in my genealogy, including Stuart, Beauchamp, Neville's and Matthew. The Matthews, a very wealthy family, owned most of the land of Glamorganshire. One ancestor, Sir David Matthew, saved the life of Edward IV, another ancestor, and there is an alabaster effigy of him in St. Mary's Chapel, located at Llandaff Cathedral outside of Cardiff.

My mother's ancestral search included early Welsh kingdoms and one 5th century monarch, King Ynyr of Gwent, including notes describing ancestors leading back to Adam, of biblical history; a long history for sure, but certainly not proven.

It was a hazy day, but the view of the castle grounds excited my historical obsession and again I felt transported back in time. It seemed to take me longer each time my mind roamed to get my bearings and return to the present. I actually had to wander back to the pub for reinforcement.

From Cardiff in the far southeast, I would head to Northwestern Wales, first stop at Conwy to see its castle and find the burial place of Prince Llewelyn, and then on to Castle Dolwyddelan in the burg of Gwynedd to see the castle Caernarfon, the home of many Welsh Princes.

In 1205, Prince Llewelyn married my great grandmother Princess Joan, daughter of King John of England. The Prince formed allies with King John and later his son, Henry III, or at least he thought they were allies. I heard a story where the Prince, known as Llewelyn the Great, captured Lord Broase and later Broase allied with the Prince and on a visit to the castle was found in the bedchambers of the Prince and in bed with his wife Joan. Llewelyn hanged Broase and the Princess was placed under house arrest and later he forgave her and she presided as Princess once more. This story seemed to haunt me.

I left Cardiff by steam train for the 159 mile journey diagonally across Wales northwest with a destination at Snowdonia National Park, where I would find the location of Prince Llewellyn's castles and fortification. The landscape in passing was at times breathtaking. From Barmouth at the southern end of Snowdonian National Park, I felt on a different planet; the ethereal views, both wild and eerily quiet, through haze and mist revealed a landscape of snow topped mountains to icy colored lakes, rugged and rocky intervals replaced by purplish moors.

I would be amiss not to mention my seat mate, Sam, a handsome Englishman. He couldn't be ignored; friendly and interesting and soon I found myself laughing along with his descriptions of life on board a train, especially one that seemed to stop for anyone along the way who might want a ride and once we thought it stopped to load up a herd of wild goats grazing on the tracks (or so it looked). As we got closer to our stop at Conwy, Sam asked if I had plans for the next day and I told him I would be looking for my great grandfather's stone casket, which I heard could be found in a parish church in a valley south of Conwy in the town of Llanrwst. Sam said he planned on renting a car and would I like to travel along with him. I told him I'd let him know. He looked safe enough, but after all was a stranger.

I had made reservations at the Castle Hotel, once an old coaching inn, located in the heart of town. The hotel stood grandly and told a tale of early days where nobles and aristocrats lodged and feasted. With all its renovation, it still held its character, including squeaky old floors. Sam wouldn't take my refusals to join him for dinner, so after a nap and cleanup we had dinner in the lovely old hotel, with very fresh local cuisine. Over glasses of Chilean wine, as local drinks seem to be more inclined to Welsh whiskey, we had a mixed seafood platter fresh from Conwy's location on the Irish Sea.

Sam Adams told me he worked on a special program with the University of Wales. Rather far from my understanding, but it involved quantum computers; something to do with qubits. He had been working in this field for the past five years after he had received a doctorate from Oxford. He was on holiday and, like me, wanted to follow his interest in castles, although he looked at them architecturally and not for 'ancestors' who lived in them. He said he had visited over a hundred so far, mostly in England and Scotland.

"Is your interest professional or past time?"

"A bit of both, but mostly a personal interest."

"It seems odd a computer scientist would have an interest in castles."

"I know, but relatives on my mother's side have a long history in England; I have castles in my heritage too."

"I wonder if your name, Adams, might be connected to the Adam's in my family tree. It seems President John Adams was a cousin of my great grandfather."

"Maybe we're cousins. My father's family is from Virginia; his father, Robert Adams, married an English girl after the war, and after receiving his architecture degree opened a firm in London. My father, Alexander Adams, now heads up the family firm."

"I thought you had a little Southern in your speech pattern."

I called James at our prescribed time and didn't get an answer. I left him my hugs and kisses. That night I dreamed about my great grandmother, Princess Joan, and her house arrest for adultery. This was a story I did not wish to relive in my dreams; but I did.

In my dream I, as Princess Joan, realized I felt fearful and repulsed by Lord Broase, who after a fortnight of wooing me, forced himself into my bedchambers after my Prince had left the castle. I felt myself crying in a cold place of isolation in the castle and wishing I could die knowing the Prince would never forgive me. One morning when I had given up all hope, the Prince came to my room, kneeled and said he believed I had not received Lord Broase into our chamber; that he was there by force. He held me in his arms. It seems a chamber maid had seen Broase enter the bedchamber and heard my cries.

The next morning, still rather in a daze from my dream, I went down for coffee and Sam joined me.

"Have you decided to travel along with me today?"

"I don't know how I could refuse; your knowledge will greatly enhance my notes about castles and hopefully get me published."

"Well, I'd rather you said you couldn't resist my charming company, but I'm here to assist. I've rented the car, it's parked out front and I'm ready to travel as soon as you are."

As we drove south in the beautiful green valley surrounded by mountains and the Irish Sea in the background, the weather, at first hazy, became brilliantly sunny, glistening off the snowy tops of the mountains. I felt as though this country far surpassed anywhere I'd been for its natural beauty. My ancestors, the early Princes of Wales, had lovely surroundings to conduct their many wars and love triangles. Sam described architectural features of castles and I took copious notes. When we reached the picturesque town of Llanrwst we found a pub and quickly downed a pint while we waited for some oysters fresh from the sea.

"I'm in love with Wales."

"It is beautiful, isn't it?"

"Cardiff looked like a nice city. Do you have family there?"

"No, I'm divorced and on my own for the past two years."

"I'm sorry."

"She decided my attention was elsewhere and we didn't share interests; both too young when we married to realize it takes more than sex to make a marriage."

"I hear you."

"At least she's remarried and there isn't any animosity between us."

The oysters came and we supped them out of the shells with a lot of lime and hot sauce, and another pint.

"Time to go find your ancestor."

"What a lovely place to reside in eternity."

We headed to the parish church to pay tribute to the last Great Prince of Wales. As we entered the parish doors, large, old and weathered, I began to feel strange, as if dream walking. I remembered reading Edward I, then king of England, a great grandfather, had ordered the Prince and his son beheaded and their heads transported to London to be placed on view at the Tower of London. I looked at the ornate stone casket and envisioned my Prince without a head.

I fainted.

Chapter Four

After I fainted, Sam carried me to a pew and the parish priest brought a wet cloth and I soon revived. Feeling embarrassed, I thanked the priest and Sam grinned all the way to the car.

"You are being insensitive."

"I'm sorry, but you seemed so helpless there before your grandfather's casket. What happened?"

"From somewhere deep within, I recalled he had been beheaded and I suddenly saw him lying there without a head."

"That would do it. I mean I understand now why you caved."

"Oh stop it."

We drove back to Conwy in quiet and I attempted to get myself back to the present; maybe this ancestor thing could be too obsessive as James had warned. It seemed I had easily become one with these ghosts.

I looked over at Sam behind the wheel, driving on the wrong side of the road, of course, and said, "I'm sorry I snapped at you. I feel foolish and embarrassed."

"Hey, don't feel embarrassed. Remember I'm also lost in time with this castle thing. It's okay, maybe we're meant to be time travelers."

"It is what it is, I guess. I wanted to ask the priest if they reunited the Prince's head with his body, but felt foolish."

"Maybe we can find out more when we get to Gwynedd."

"We?"

"Hey, you don't intend to dump me before we get to the end of the trail?"

He told me he would be going back to Cardiff after visiting Gwynedd and castle Caernarfon and since I would be going back into England before heading for Scotland, where I intended to spend the rest of the year, he thought at least we could spend our last days together.

"Okay, you've made your case and I do need more input about castles, and who knows, I might be in for more ghost travelling and need someone to revive me."

"I'm your Lancelot."

"Oh no, where in the world did that come from, I didn't mention him did I?"

"No, I don't think so. It just seemed the thing to say. Why the hair trigger?"

I told him about my dream in regard to King Arthur after visiting Tintagel Castle. He laughed some more and thought we definitely had become fellow time travelers.

"Okay, my Prince, but let's leave it in the past."

"Your wish my command, dear Guinevere."

Back at the hotel I took a long bath, even falling asleep at one point, dreaming of a wild black dog chasing a headless horseman across the moor. It seemed I couldn't escape my dreams. I dried off and grabbed a small bottle of Welsh whiskey from the mini-bar in the room. It tasted pretty good. I had another over ice. Dressed and ready for dinner I joined Sam in the lobby and he said he'd made reservations at a restaurant on the upper coast, supposedly a not to miss when in Conwy County. Off we went on another beautiful drive arriving on the peninsula above Conwy on the north Irish Sea. The restaurant sat us with a table overlooking the water and we dined in elegance with lovely wine and three courses of to die for fresh food, from oysters to sea bass to rich dessert. Carlos, in Llandudo, is a must stop for anyone visiting in this region.

"Thank you for bringing me to this wonderful place. You promised we'd go Dutch so let me pick this up and if we dine together tomorrow night, you can pick up that tab."

"I got this one covered; you can get the next one."

I slept like a rock that night—no dreams. Maybe I'll overcome this dilemma, I thought.

Early the next morning Sam joined me for a full English breakfast of thick bacon, fresh eggs and toast with marmalade and then we headed out for Conwy Castle, built by King Edward I, (a great grandfather) between 1283-89, after his conquest of Wales, and the beheading of my great grandfather Llewellyn, Prince of Wales. The great structure included the walled city of Comwy. Sam said this was the greatest example of late thirteenth century military architecture in Europe. King Henry VIII did restoration work in the 1530's where it was used as a depot, a prison and residence for visitors. It is now a World Heritage site.

We spent hours walking about the old castle, including getting to the watchtower where you could see the Irish Sea coastline. The royal rooms were positioned on the first floor and well protected by walls and facing the courtyard. I could see King Edward with his wife Eleanor of Castile, daughter of King Ferdinand III of Castile, and their many children, including their daughter, Joan Plantagenet, another great grandmother. As I considered ancestors, Sam found this castle a feast for his study of medieval architecture. I wondered what we would find tomorrow in Gwynedd.

That evening to get even with Sam's great choice for dinner the night before, I made reservations at Signatures located near the Conwy Marina. I had heard some good reviews; courses with sorbet in between, delicious and good atmosphere. I thought it sounded like a good place to say goodbye to Conwy.

"Where you taking me, my Lady?"

"For your pleasure, I'm sure, dear Lancelot."

"Here we go—a couple of time travelers into the woods for dinner."

"Silly. It's not in the woods, but by the marina. Onwards in your iron steed, Sir."

When we first entered the lovely dark woodsy atmosphere (maybe woods after all), we heard Frank Sinatra singing in the lounge. We quickly peeked in and saw a ruddy Welshman singing *My Way;* so nice to hear this soft, swinging music instead of a Lady Gaga imitator. Another sign I lived for my mother's time and her preferred swing jazz sounds.

The red bow tied waiter took us to a special table overlooking the water and a view of the marina and its many boats. We ordered a wonderful seafood risotto with a white sparkling wine and then changed to Beaujolais with local lamb prepared two ways, both delicious. Several miniature vegetables and homemade rolls accompanied the entre and we still couldn't refuse a sticky toffee pudding for dessert.

"You chose well."

"Thank you. I think so too."

We stopped by the lounge at the Castle Hotel and had a Welsh whiskey for a night cap. I looked at my watch and I needed to place my call to James, so we said good night and looked forward to visiting the last castle of the last Prince on the last day in Wales.

The next morning Sam decided he would keep the car and drive to Caernarfon through what is known as the Old Kingdom of Gwynredd, a sparsely populated, mountainous region of northwest Wales, and since the 12th century, home to the Llewellyn's, Princes of Wales.

Sam chatted as he drove, "It's a little over an hour drive through some of the grandest scenery we've seen yet, so they say."

"I hear we'll be close to the highest mountain in Wales."

"Yes, Mount Eryri, the highest peak in the Snowdon range. The walled old city of Caernarfon where the large scale castle is located is nearby. Have you made reservations?"

"I made them last night at the Black Boy Inn, which is within the walled city and walking distance to the castle. And you?"

"Amazing, me too and the same reason; I also understand they have a popular pub."

The drive, as Sam described, held me breathless and once again I wondered why in all my years I'd not been told of the grandeur of this land. I came to the United Kingdom to view castles, but now I understood castle building was about location, and in this case they had mountain ranges for refuse in face of invasion, abundant water for transportation of goods and fallow land for harvesting. This land of my ancestors had it all.

I checked into the quaint old Inn and found a clean room with a comfortable bed. I met Sam in the pub for lunch. We both enjoyed crisp fish and chips, a couple ales, and finally started our castle tour. Sam felt a group tour on day one, would give me a better idea of what to see and he could add his two cents worth. The guide told us the early Roman fortress had been in the hands of many warring factions over the years. It stood on a large scale, including its walled city, at the mouth of the Seiont River. The early Welsh Kings lived here beginning in 1115, and they ruled Gwynedd and southern areas until their kingdom fell to King Edward I in 1283. His son Edward II was born at the castle, and became England's first Prince of Wales. Charles is the present day Prince of Wales. Edward I and II, as stated earlier, were both great grandfathers.

Sam's architectural interests proved to be the key for my book research. I learned castles, from early Roman to late Edwardian, held many differentiated architectural features; from motes to mounds, from towers to turrets. This day we walked miles up turrets, across walls, down towers into courtyards, through royal accommodations and ancient gardens. I took down as many notes as possible so I would have material for the book I planned to write over the winter in Scotland.

It felt good to be back at the Inn. I napped for about an hour and then took a leisurely shower before dressing for dinner. I met Sam at the bar where we had another Welsh whiskey, beginning to like this manly drink—and decided we'd try dining at Jake's Bistro, which everyone said we shouldn't miss. It's location down a historic street with its nicely restored white façade with dark green trim seemed welcoming and inside the warm atmosphere of wood and light added to feeling good about our choice. We had been advised by management to bring our own wine, if we preferred it, and they served it without corkage. You can tell how good the food is by its customers and although this was a week night, it didn't have an empty table.

I decided I wanted their pate for starters and Sam ordered a risotto. I wanted more of the delicious fresh bass and Sam remembered how he loved the lamb dish. We felt the Italian Prosecco would go with both. I thought Sam and I seemed like a compatible married couple and thought how strange is that. We chatted, laughed and enjoyed about everything about our travels. I knew it had come time to leave this handsome, square jawed man with the dark blond wavy hair behind. He had become a bit too comfortable.

"I'm going to stay on for a couple more days; so much for me to discover here."

"I understand—we barely touched on your architectural interests today."

"Are you headed out tomorrow?"

"Yes, I have reservations on the bus to Brighton at ten. I've decided to stay there and travel to the castle at Arundel, built by Henry I."

"Another grandfather?"

"Of course," laughing at the pretend look on his face of haughty resignation;

"It's the present home of the Duke and Duchess of Norfolk and is full of treasures from great paintings, tapestries to stained glass. Other names abound here too, like Henry II and the Fitz Alan's—which mother identified as ancestors. Queen Victoria liked to stay here."

"A relative?"

"No, looks like I missed out there."

"She was a bit stocky to be your relative. How tall are you, 5'3"? And, I must add, about 110 lbs. of perfectly put together structure with lovely reddish brown hair surrounding an oval face set with a perfectly shaped nose, lovely lips and large brown eyes."

"Good god, you describe me as if I were one of your castles."

"No, just observant of perfection."

"Okay silly, thanks, I think, for the compliment. I've enjoyed doing Wales with you and I'll miss you from now on. But at least you've taught me what to look for when I travel to more castles."

"Call me once in a while, will you? I'm beginning to feel like Lancelot when Guinevere went back to King Arthur."

"But I never left my King Arthur, he is only back at our castle."

"Well, you accompanied me in my iron steed. If you have any problems or need some assistance, remember I'm a native Londoner and can always help you out."

We stood, he gave me a warm hug and gentle kiss on my cheek and we parted.

Chapter Five

S am came to the bus to wish me bon voyage, and as I left him in the rear view mirror (Texan talk), I missed my Lancelot already. Today I thought I might be lucky and have a seat to myself, but then came this long haired young man with backpack. By his odor he probably hadn't bathed since he left home, (somewhere in the States long ago). He looked stoned and soon fell asleep. I decided right there and then I would get off earlier than planned, instead of going to Brighton and back to Arundel to see the castle, I would get off in Arundel; about 150 miles in the distance. I used my trusty international smart phone to cancel reservations in Brighton and made new reservations for the night at the Norfolk Arms Hotel, a Georgian coaching inn, in Arundel.

I thought about stopping in Cheshire, a village along the route, to visit Beeston Castle, now mostly in ruins, where Henry III and his son Edward I, set up their base for the campaign against the Welsh Princes. I had such sentiment for the Welsh Princes, and anger at Edward I for displaying the Last Prince's head at the Tower of London, I decided I'd leave the place in its solitude.

The Midlands and South East England looked splendid in early spring; beautiful gardens surrounding darling little white cottages, city parks and small country lanes. The fields of green would change to fields of yellow and then fields of blue. Again I wanted to get my easel and paint in plein air. I used my camera instead, and perhaps someday I could try to paint the vision; knowing I would lack the atmosphere and awe of original inspiration.

Arriving in Arundel, in South East England, I dropped off my bags at the hotel and walked to the Tea Garden at the Waterside, a restaurant on the river. I ordered their famous cream tea and a sandwich. The weather ideal and sunny, temperature in mid-70's; perfect spring weather. I listened to the clanging of the sail boat masts and marveled at the various colors of the motor boats; another perfect picturesque setting and more photos for my collection.

As I walked about, I loved this small village located in the South Downs of West Sussex with population of around 3000. It had a picturesque setting on the river Arun, which before the railroad, brought goods and materials from the coast, five miles away, to the port of Arundel. In the early days it had a large market and annual fair where people from all around bought and sold their wares. The town is set off by a conservation area of historic buildings; many of the old timber houses now have new facades but the town still reflects its medieval history. There is a beautiful parish church and a magnificent looking cathedral, reflecting pink in the sunlight.

The centerpiece of the town is the medieval castle whose massive presence stands in control of the landscape. Henry I, son of William the Conqueror, had been crowned here in 1100, and he and my grandmother Edith Matilda, lived here along with their son Stephen, who would follow Henry to the crown; after Stephen, my grandfather Henry II and my grandmother Eleanor of Aquitaine did more building on the castle and later it fell into the hands of Fitz Alan's (in my ancestry), Howard's and Boleyn's. Henry VIII with his wife Ann Boleyn spent time here and it also was a favorite for Queen Victoria. It presently is the home of the Duke and Duchess of Norfolk. In checking further into my ancestry, I found great grandmother Lady Alice Fitz Alan, Countess of Kent, had been born in the castle in 1350, daughter of Count Richard the 9th Fitz Alan and Eleanor

Plantagenet, Countess of Arundel. Alice was the grandmother of James Stewart I, King of Scotland (a grandfather). I would locate him later in the Palace Dunfermline, Fife, Scotland.

Castle Arundel had a moat and a 100 foot mound and sat on 40 acres. I needed Sam to describe the type of castle, but I felt from all the notes I had from him, I would be able to formulate a description of the architecture for my book. I arrived at the castle just in time for the afternoon tour, so I joined in. Once again you need to be a Billy goat to climb all the towers, walk across the walls and descend into the rooms of the royals. The more I see of castles, unlike churches, the more I'm ready to see the next one. That's good since I've dedicated this year to those homes of medieval ancestors. I took a copious amount of notes because I didn't have Sam to fall back on.

I went back to the river for dinner at Waterside, as it was a warm evening and they had outside seating overlooking the boats and sparkling lights reflecting in the water. I had a bass filet once again as I hadn't had a bad fish dish in England, accompanied by a delicious vegetable stuffing so very fresh and properly cooked. I sipped a couple glasses of Sauvignon Blanc.

The next day, after arriving in Brighton, I checked into the Marine View, a family run hotel I had read about. It is located so each room has a view of the sea and Brighton Pier, which reminded me of the pier in Santa Monica; bright carnival lights, Ferris wheel and fun for everyone; the perfect location for walking and visiting the nearby Garden Square, so wonderful in the spring. I rested for a while, then showered and headed out to make my reservations to see the castles on the following two days.

After my nap I walked out on the pier, enjoying all the frivolity, walked along the waterfront and viewed the large assortment of boats, including yachts that would look at home in Monaco (and maybe were). I stopped at Brighton Shellfish and Oyster Bar located on the long, sandy beach, for deliciously fresh oysters and a pint and then decided to visit the Oriental stylized Brighton Pavilion. Loved or hated for its style, it has attracted visitors for over 200 years. It is described as a fantasy skyline of domes and minarets; the Chinese style had become popular in England in the 18th century. It was in reality a royal palace for Prince George IV, redesigned over time until its present look. You entered into a grand hall and then into main rooms off the hall and then the Prince's apartment. The rooms are full of color, gilding and oriental figures, tapestry and paintings. I found it very eye appealing, although somewhat out of contrast with castles.

It is said an air of supreme elegance pervades throughout this lovely old town, and as I walked about I could see what is meant; Regency Square is known for some of the finest domestic architecture in the country. They say built when style mattered. I had debated not coming to Brighton, perhaps instead going directly to Dover, but now I knew I had made the right choice; it had attracted famous people to its place of culture, including Dickens and Oscar Wilde, and if you like churches, you would love the 800 year old St. Helen's Church. Brighton had theatre, museums and seafaring history; what more could you ask for.

Back at my hotel, I rested and decided to make reservations at English's of Brighton; several fellow travelers advised me of its fresh and delicious menu. The restaurant is located in The Lanes, the oldest quarter of town lined with fishermen's cottages from the 17th century. On a cobblestone street with decorative iron lamp poles whose light glistened off old Edwardian façades, I found English's. Upon entering I was greeted by warmth and charm. The restaurant is famous for its seafood, especially oysters, so I started with a glass of Bellini Prosecco and a plate of Oysters Rockefeller, followed by Scallops St. Jacques and more Prosecco. Not quite saturated I finished with an espresso crème Brule. It was a lovely meal, every mouthful a delight.

Early the next morning I had a continental breakfast before I caught the bus for the short trip to Lewes. I got out of the bus and with others headed for the castle located in the center of town, I heard someone say, "Leah, Leah, hello."

I looked around and saw Tom and Amy walking towards me. "I can't believe my eyes, how good to see you again."

"We came down for the week to see Lewes and a couple other castles before heading to Brighton for the weekend."

"That's where I'm staying."

"What hotel?"

I told them and found out they had reservations not far from me. We walked along together to the castle and joined the tour. Lewes castle is rare, they say, because of two moats. I imagined Sam had already visited this rarity. It was built by William de Warenne in 1067, on land given to him by Duke William of Normandy, known as William the Conqueror, both names in my mother's genealogy. We climbed to the top of the 14ᵗʰ century magnificent barbican (a fortified gateway) and shell keep (a type of castle)—needed Sam again for all this terminology.

Lewes is located by the River Ouse, on a hillside between the river and the castle. The streets rise steeply and High Street is lined with Georgian shops. We found a pub and relaxed over fish and chips and a couple pints each. Seeing Amy and Tom again delighted me, almost like seeing old lost friends, but they were new found friends.

"Do you like Brighton?"

"Very much; the seafood has been to die for and the beach, marina and pier are people packed, and I've enjoyed milling around with everyone."

"Don't you love the town itself? We always find new sites of interest as we walk around the streets."

"Yes, the town is lovely. I had dinner last night in The Lanes, in a wonderful old English restaurant."

"You must mean English's of Brighton. It is famous. I'm glad you found it. Was the food just marvelous?"

"Absolutely. Looks like time for me to find my bus. Maybe we can get together in Brighton?"

"We'll call you tomorrow and see if we can have dinner together; maybe seafood on the beach. We want to hear all about your trip through Wales."

I joined the line heading for the bus and grabbed a few winks as we headed back to Brighton.

After resting and a shower I headed back to The Lanes for dinner at Ole Ole, a highly recommended Tapa Bar and Restaurant. I ordered the set menu of tapa's and paella with sangria. They brought a pitcher (instead of glass) of the red wine with fruit marinated in brandy. Good thing I had a taxi ride home. On top of the sangria and delicious food, I enjoyed some really fine flamenco dancing. The bar was alive with merry patrons enjoying a night out. It would have been fun if Tom and Amy had been with me, but I managed to join a group of reveling Canadians, who made me feel one of them.

The next morning, with a slight hangover, I had coffee and just a complimentary taste of the full English breakfast offered by the hotel. Feeling somewhat revived, I headed to the bus where I found a rather subdued group of passengers (including the Canadians from the night before) headed out for Pevensey. It seems Friday night revelry had left its mark.

Pevensey Castle originally sat next to the Sussex Sea, where its location made it an important fortress for Romans. It is the landing place of William the Conqueror, Duke of Normandy, in 1066. After the sea receded and the harbor on which it was built became filled up, the Normans still found it to be an important fortification and William gave the castle to his half-brother, Count of Mortain, who reinforced its importance by surrounding it with a moat, and adding to its structure of curtain walls and round towers. Instead of a rectangular castle of the times, it was built on an oval, more open plan. I add this description thinking of Sam and his expertise in castle design. Although it is now in ruins, the moat and crumbling remains are still very impressive.

An interesting note about Pevensey Castle is it is a favorite of ghost hunters; they've seen a grey lady and man, a little drummer boy, a hundred Roman soldiers, a young girl and her dog and I suppose other images have appeared over the years. I'm told you can join a ghost walk on certain Saturday nights. Think I'll pass on that; I've enough ghosts of my own.

After our castle tour we drove to the seaside town of Eastbourne to grab some lunch at a pub. In the 10th century the 7th Duke of Devonshire first expanded and developed the genteel little town on the sea. The town has many Victorian homes and gardens, and is a favorite location for artists and sailors of all kinds. Next we drove about two miles to see Beachy Head, where dramatic white cliffs rise high out of the channel with the candy striped lighthouse below. The sight left me breathless, no wonder it is such an iconic coastal view in Britain.

Chapter Six

That evening, back in Brighton, I found a bistro and ordered coq au vin and a glass of white Bordeaux. The chicken dish tasted as though it had been slow cooked for hours. I loved it. Feeling contented, I ambled back to my hotel, gave James a call and once again it went to message. I left hugs and kisses and asked, "Where are you without me?" I slept in the next morning and had coffee and scones in my room, delivered by the gracious staff. I decided to write and my trusty lap top felt new beneath my fingers—it had been a long time since I had worked on the book and I had many notes to transcribe from my time with Sam until the present.

The phone rang about noon and Amy said, "Can you meet us for lunch?"

"Give me about thirty and I'll be on my way. Where will I find you?"

"Let's meet at the Town Hall; we want to try Japanese food for a change. Does that sound okay with you?

"Love it, see you soon."

I met them and we went to Moshi Moshi a popular Japanese restaurant in Bartholomew Square, with a very unique futuristic décor. Amy and Tom had made a good choice; we ordered bento boxes with

Japanese beer. It was a nice change and the sushi was delicious and I could have eaten more of the vegetable tempura, so light and fresh.

"So Leah, how did you like Wales?"

"Where can I begin; for one thing it is so very beautiful with its contrasts from high mountains, lakes and moors. I took the steam train from Cardiff to Conwy in the Snowdonian National Park. I realized my ancestors lived an isolated, but privileged existence in this wild country."

"We've not visited the park area yet; need to put it on our itinerary."

"You won't be sorry. I could go back a thousand times. Aside from the scenery, the castles located in the mountainous areas, or on the Irish Sea, are massive and imposing. They offered the Prince's great defense."

"How about the accommodations?"

"Couldn't have been more pleased; when you're ready to visit, give me a call and I'll recommend some of the places I stayed and some great places to dine."

"Did you join tours to see the castles?"

"Yes, in most part, although I was lucky to meet a fellow traveler on the train from Cardiff who also had an obsession with castles. He, however, was not looking for the ghosts of ancestors but castle construction. Since I'm planning on writing a book about castles, he helped me understand what to look for and I've amassed a trove of notes."

Is he Welsh?"

"No, English from London, although his father is native to Virginia married to his English mother. He is a computer scientist studying something in regard to quantum computers, based in Cardiff. His name is Sam Adams, another name in my mother's genealogy. His father is an architect in London, Randolph Adams, perhaps you've heard of him?"

"Oh yes. A very prominent family, his wife is a Belford; so you met a shirt sleeve cousin?"

"Looks that way; he rented a car in Conwy and offered to drive me to a small town in the Conwy valley to visit a parish where Prince Llewellyn's casket resides. The countryside is breathtaking. We visited the castles together and also dined at some nice restaurants."

"No kissing cousin stuff?"

I laughed and said, "Of course not" and we changed the subject.

After dinner we walked to the pier and watched the crowds and enjoyed the bright lights and sounds. Brighton certainly had been a nice place to spend a few days, but now I needed to get on with my travels. Once again Amy and Tom said they would look for me at other destinations and we said our goodbyes.

The next morning I caught my bus to Dover. I looked forward to those high white cliffs I had heard so much about over the years. I can remember my mother singing, *"The White Cliffs of Dover"* about bluebirds returning after the bombing of London was over. I remember it had a lovely melody and I loved to hear her sing; as then I knew she had "a song in her heart" and it made me happy, as her life had been difficult.

I checked into the Dover Marina Hotel with its lovely Regency décor. My trusty guide book indicated its location perfect for walking to the center of town and the seaport. I grabbed an early lunch at the hotel's restaurant and scheduled the tour to Dover Castle for the next day and as I had not had some real good exercise for a while, decided to use the paths provided for a coastal walk above the cliffs. The breeze, so fresh from the sea, brought a charge of energy through my being. Most of my life I have been recharged by my contact with the sea; those negative ions seemed to make all things promising and possible. After returning to town, I stopped and had tea time at Mrs. Knott's Tea Room to enhance my British adventure and then walked around Russell Gardens with spring flowers, shrubs and plants richly displayed and saw Dover Castle looming large on historic Castle

Street. I stopped by the Dover Museum where I enjoyed the history of the seaport; the largest and busiest in England, where ferries and sea craft carry visitors back and forth from England to France and where cruise ships of all sizes are berthed. Tired, I returned to my hotel for a nap.

Since I craved a change of taste from the usual local cuisine, I realized I would love a pasta dish. I'd heard of Dinos Italian Restaurant on Castle Street, which had a view of the night lit Dover Castle, and made reservations for the evening. I arrived around eight and a charming waiter sat me at small table located along the wall close to the bar. I smiled at the many wine bottles in their baskets hanging from the ceiling. The walls painted in a rich golden color held paintings with Italian scenes, and the tables dressed in white, seemed elegant in a somewhat dated décor. I ordered an Italian red with my starter of escargot, which I hadn't had in ages; I loved its garlicky sauce, which I drenched with my Italian bread. I switched to a glass of Chianti with my Spaghetti al Pomodoro, a tasty sauce of tomato, garlic and basil. I felt very satisfied, but decided to top it off with a lemon sorbet.

The walk back to the hotel helped digest my dinner and I received a call on my cell just as I entered my room.

"Hello."

"Hi there my fair lady; thought I'd call before you put in your nightly call to James."

"You got me just home from a superb Italian dinner; how nice to hear your voice."

"Yours too; I've been thinking about you. Have you been getting around okay without your trusty companion?"

"In fact your knowledge of castles has helped me so much. I'm here in Dover now and will see the castle tomorrow and then take a bus to Leeds to see that castle."

"What other castles have you seen?"

"After leaving you that early morning, I stopped at Arundel for a day and visited the Castle Arundel, then on to Brighton for three days where

I took buses to visit Castle Lewes and Castle Pevensey. I'm so proud I've been able to take notes of some quality for my book; thanks to you."

"You've been busy; where to after Kent?"

"I'm really thinking of cutting across to Cumbria and visiting Appleby Castle, the home of Clifford ancestors, and then to Castle Carlisle. From there I'll head to Durham, as my paternal grandmother's maiden name was Durham and several earlier ancestor came from that region and then Barnard Castle, which includes names in my genealogy; Balliol, Neville, Beauchamp, King John and Edward I, and then on to Northumberland to visit Castle Bamburgh and perhaps others I need to research."

"Wow, you are staying busy. I thought I might get away to visit with you when you get to Scotland. I need to make a trip to Edinburgh one of these days. Any chance you know when you might be there?"

"I plan on going to Edinburgh when I leave Northumberland, but haven't formulated a timeline yet."

"Why don't you give me a call when you know when you'll head for Edinburgh and I'll make plans to join you for a few days? I'd be a great guide to Edinburgh Castle."

"I'll call you and your guidance would be appreciated; I've missed it."

"Not missing your humble knight?"

"Silly. You're not humble."

After talking with Sam, I called James and brought him up-to-date on my whereabouts. He said he'd been busy and sorry he had missed my calls; he had visiting scholars in for the month and had been busy with them. I asked if he thought he could get away in a month or so when I would be writing in Scotland and he thought he probably could, but it would be later before he would know for sure. Maybe it was just my own uncertainty, but his voice seemed more remote than usual. Well, after all I had left him for this obsessive journey in the guise of publishing to meet my professorship responsibilities. Then again I really needed to publish and this history fit my curriculum. I didn't want to feel guilty about it.

Chapter Seven

The next morning I joined the tour to Dover Castle, one of the largest castles in the country located on the closest crossing point to the European continent. William the Conqueror added to what had been a site since the Iron Age, a light house and church, but Henry II set the blueprints for the existing castle and King John completed its defenses. During World War II it became a hospital and a command center for the Dunkirk evacuation. The castle sits high above the White Cliffs with a spectacular view of the port and the sea beyond. The site is very hilly, so it helps to be a mountain goat (Capricorn). We saw medieval tunnels and later the secret tunnels built during the war years. The Great Tower, richly garnered with vivid colors and opulence, became the royal court of Henry II and his wife Eleanor of Aquitaine. We heard about the ghostly presence and gossip in the castle about how Henry's sons plotted to take over the empire.

I enjoyed the tour and all the stories and intrigues, especially knowing each name existed on my family tree, but I mostly enjoyed the vast view from those heights; the magnificent white cliffs and realizing its closeness to France. The fog of my reality again seemed lost in past history, as I vividly recalled the ghosts of Henry II and Eleanor walking these halls.

I had a light dinner at the hotel and decided to go to the room and work on my notes and do some research about Leeds and its castle I'd see tomorrow, about a ten mile trip I'd take by local bus.

That night the dreams came back with great intensity.

I heard the voice of Henry II, "You will be imprisoned for taking the side of our sons."

Being Eleanor of Aquitaine, I responded, "They would not have deceived you, if you'd only listened to them, you have been stubborn and a bully to them."

"Hush, you're lucky I don't take your head."

With that Eleanor, a great beauty and mother of five future kings of England, went into house arrest for six years. And then in a continuing dream as Eleanor, I knew of all of Henry's affairs with women over the years, and how he seemed to be totally smitten by Rosamund Clifford. When she died suspiciously, the rumors spread of how I had poisoned her. I laughed because my wish would have been to poison Henry.

Once again I found it difficult to wake to my reality. Strong coffee and a hot shower seemed to help.

I found my bus to Leeds and with a bus full of happy and noisy tourists; we headed for Leeds Castle sitting on 500 acres of parkland in the midst of a lake. One of the most beautiful castles in England, so they said, and we all agreed it was a spectacular sight. The castle was given by King Edward I to his wife Eleanor of Castile, again grandparents, and it became the couple's favorite retreat, and the home of six queens to follow. The sun glistened off the surrounding moat and waters under another cloudless sky, which I felt so thankful to discover, after everyone warned me of the rainy, gray days I would encounter on my trip.

Inside, the library is lined from ceiling to flour with books and the dining room set for a king. The décor remained reminiscent of King Edward's reign and I allowed myself to feel his and Eleanor's presence in these great halls. Although I had resentment of Edward

I, due to his war that allowed for the beheading of my great grandfather, the last true Prince of Wales, I had to realize he also was a grandfather and I had to admire his taste for grandeur. It was a long and tiring tour, but I left feeling the wonder of time past.

On the tour bus back to Dover everyone seemed to nod off, including me. I drifted in my foggy state back to the 13th century and I became my grandmother, Eleanor of Castile sitting at my large ornate desk in bedchambers contemplating my happy marriage to Edward. Remembering how my father, King Ferdinand III of Castile, and Edward's father, King Henry III, arranged our marriage to align Spain with England. What they got was an alignment of great love and fidelity, until death do we part.

I had a light dinner at the hotel restaurant, retired early thinking I'd call James once I arrived in Appleby-in-Westmorland the next evening.

I enjoyed the train trip to Appleby-in-Westmorland on the river Eden with the variety of views of the English countryside. It so happened to be the first rainy day I'd encountered. The depot in Appleby seemed to be a photographer's dream, as many steam engine trains visited there. My guide book said this town "is stunningly beautiful" and they didn't exaggerate. The Castle, which is now private to the public, is sited at the head of Main Street; the home of Clifford's for over 400 years and Lady Ann Clifford lived here and her name is associated widely in historic places. What make this such a wondrous land are the rolling countryside of the Yorkshire Moors on one side, and the majestic peaks of the Lake District on the other side. It is said this is England at its best, even on a rainy day.

I had made reservations at Royal Oak Appleby, a traditional 17th century coaching inn. After the three hour trip I felt hungry, so I stopped at a village pub and ordered a lager and lime at the bar and from the menu at the small table I ordered pork pie and chips; a yummy pie made from many parts of the pig, including bacon, plus carrots, celery, onions, pepper, salt and nutmeg. The good-looking waiter gave me the menu. I love the atmosphere of these English pubs; we have a few "Irish" pubs where I live, but nothing compares to the real thing. Although the English are thought of as reserved it seems in the pub atmosphere they are warm and hospitable.

All filled up, I rested in my room for a couple hours, writing down notes and reviewing things to do in this beautiful county. I found out the castle would not be open for tours, so made reservations to see Carlisle Castle, an English Heritage site, the next day and decided to spend the afternoon looking around town. Appleby is situation in a valley of the River Eden and is noted for its walking tours. It is an historic market town known as the location for Gypsy horse sales; they now arrive each June in modern recreational vehicles instead of their original caravans of horse drawn colorful covered wagons. Once again I recalled a song my mother liked to sing *Golden Earrings* from a movie about gypsies; I'd always loved it and dreamed of being a lovely gypsy girl by a campfire, with my lover admiring my golden earrings. Over the years I've enjoyed wearing looped earrings of gold.

That evening as I entered the lobby of the Inn, I saw a lady I'd met on the train. Anna was from California and we had struck it up as interested travelers. We decided to have dinner together at Ashiana, a nearby Asian Restaurant that had been recommended. I ordered an Indian lamb dish with rice and flat bread. We ordered a Rose, which went good with the spicy food.

Anna had recently gone through a divorce from a pretty well-known producer in Hollywood and decided she wanted to see the world. So far she had travelled to Rome and Florence, spent a month in Venice and planned on going to Amsterdam and Scandinavia after a month's stay in London. I thought she was probably in her early fifties, had classic features and lovely red hair, probably not her natural color. She said she had not been lucky enough to have children and had always wanted to travel, but her husband, she said without bitterness, travelled only for business and didn't want the distraction of her presence on locations.

"Was it an amicable divorce?"

"As much as you could expect in Hollywood; I came into the marriage with money and managed to at least get my own assets back. He fought me in regard to what he thought he earned, but, of course, California is a 50-50 state on earnings made after marriage, much to his chagrin."

"I'm glad you're beginning to live your dreams."

"Where are you off to next?"

"I've train reservation in the morning to Carlisle on the Scottish-English border where I'll stay for a few days before heading to Durham and Northumberland. My final destination for the fall and winter will be somewhere in Scotland where I can find a quiet, remote place to write; haven't decided where for sure."

"I'm going back to London to visit with some friends who will be joining me for a month or so. Geoffrey and I share a town house in London and I'm looking forward to seeing friends again."

We exchanged cards and said our good night.

The next morning, I took the steam train to Carlisle, only 30 miles distance. My love of train travel growing with each experience. The station, located in town center of Carlisle and walking distance to my hotel, the lovely Victorian Hallmark, offered my first view of this town which for over 1700 years had occupied an important position on the border of two countries. The Carlisle Castle has stood in silent witness for over nine hundred years of history, is now in ruins except for gateways and the tower. Edward I held his parliament here and other lasting impressions are from Mary, Queen of Scots, Bonnie Prince Edward and Sir Walter Scott who was married here, of the above only Edward is on my family tree. The castle sits imposing itself over the town, with many stairways and secret chambers and dungeons. Carlisle itself is a place for business and a stopping place for travel to and from Scotland. It's known for horse racing and fine blooded horses, and has excellent accommodations and the finest of restaurants. The area itself is close to the Lake District National Park, Hadrian's Wall and within a few miles distance you'll find sparkling lakes, tumbling waterfalls and high peaks.

After checking into the Hallmark and making reservations to tour the castle the next day, I went out for a walk about. I loved the Victorian ambiance and walking amongst the homes I felt transported back in time. The Lanes, a shopping mecca, had many lovely shops to buy or browse. By lunch time I found a bistro offering tapas and I stopped in and enjoyed five different selections, all delicious, and a good house red wine. I usually don't like squid, but this fried squid proved me wrong and although I eat very little red meat, the dish of steak strips made up for any lack of red blood, and I gave thanks to the cow for her sacrifice.

I walked faster and further to help ward off excess calories, knowing I'd made reservations at one of Carlisle's best restaurants for dinner. I remembered I'd promised frugality on this trip, but I also knew my journey might eventually lead to a travel book. I wondered if my delusions went further than just dreaming of ancestors, perhaps I was making a cover story to support my gluttony.

I stopped by Tullie House museum and art gallery in a large red brick Jacobean mansion. I enjoyed their fine art collection of mostly English art from present back to about 1650. Aside from paintings, oils and watercolor, they exhibited many sculptures, drawings and prints. I thought of my blank canvas on the easel back home in my 'studio'. When would I get inspired to paint again? I wondered.

Next, I went to the Carlisle Cathedral and marveled at this medieval cathedral located on this site for over 900 years. Worship is still offered here daily and I thought, surrounded by the beauty of its stained glass arched windows, adorned ceilings reaching to heaven, many candles and magnificence, I could well attend to my soul needs here.

Thinking of my souls needs, I decided to go back to the hotel, grab a nap and get ready for dinner at eight at David's, a top rated restaurant in town. I dressed for dinner, putting on my finest, and since a light rain had started, I hailed a taxi to the Victorian Townhouse in the historic center of town. Asked who I would be joining, I graciously said I'd be dining alone and the stiff necked maître di seated me in an inconspicuous location. I smiled and thanked him in spite of his rude behavior. But none the less, I found the atmosphere charming and I ordered a gin martini, something I hadn't done thus far; and would do more often, realizing this British gin reminiscent of all things royal. Or so I felt.

I ordered a seafood terrine for starters, followed by roast breast of duck, accompanied by an Argentine Malbec. For desert I ordered a plum and gin sorbet with a strong cup of coffee, to help with the chilly, rainy weather. My curly headed waiter made up for the aloofness of the maître di, so I tipped him generously and he gave me his most charming smile. The glories of youth, I thought.

I slept well, in spite of the strong coffee and arose to another rainy day. I dressed in rain garb, grabbed my umbrella and stopped in the hotel café for a quick breakfast before taking a taxi to the castle, where I would meet my tour group. About twenty tourists arrived in spite of the rain and the tour guide looked like a school girl; again the glories of youth. She told us the castle began as a Roman fortress and today it houses a military museum. The castle keep, or great tower, displayed the long history of its prominence in history and commanded the strongholds skyline; the keep is four stories high and has a roof platform. Henry I ordered the castle be built here, but probably didn't see much progress by the time of his death in 1135. It is thought the keep was completed after Scottish occupation by David I. (Yes, Grandfather David) and I realized how over the years the Scots and English fought their wars of dominance. When the guide spoke of its architectural complexity I thought of Sam and realized he had probably been here. There are murals in relief and carvings and it isn't known when they were done, or by whom, but by their depictions, it is thought around 1460 during the time of the Percy's.

A couple from Boston joined me for the tour through the military museum. They said they wanted to see Carlisle before heading for Dumfries in Scotland where they would visit the home of Robert Burns. Gordon taught English and loved Burns. We talked about

Robert the Bruce, King of Scotland, who I would be including in my Scotland days and we wondered how true the movie *Braveheart* had been to history. Dorothy said her ancestry led to Northern Ireland in the 1700's and she guessed they probably came from Scotland, but didn't have any information. They asked me if I'd like to join them for dinner; they wanted to try a new place. I agreed readily.

Gordon and Dorothy didn't drink alcohol, so we enjoyed some very healthy green tea along with a nice menu at Runes Thai Restaurant. I ordered spring rolls for a starter and then a cup of clear vegetable and noodle soup. The main consisted of chicken in curry paste cooked with coconut milk and pineapple; very refreshing on my palate, spicy hot but not too. Gordon loved to talk about 'Rabbie' Burns and I loved his easy way of bringing you along. I didn't know "*Auld Lang Syne*" was attributed to Burns but had heard of his poem about a red rose and suddenly off of Gordon's Scottish tongue;

Oh my luve's a red red rose, that's newly sprung in June;
Oh, my luve's like the melodie, that's sweetly played in tune.

He continued with two other verses, ending with;

And fare thee well, my only Luve, and fare thee well, a while!
And I will come again, my Luve, tho' it were ten thousand miles.

I sat transfixed and felt certain I'd never heard anything so beautiful in my whole life. "Gordon, how very lovely—you brought Burns alive for me."

"Thank you. I've taught him for years, and this trip to see his home and a walk in his footsteps is a dream of a lifetime."

That night I sat and wrote about the castle and with Burn's in my mind, decided to call James early in chance of catching him. His call went to message, so without a second thought I dialed Sam's number.

"Hi Sam."

"Hi there, my lady."

"I just had such a lovely evening, I had to share it and James isn't home."

"Wow, am I always your second choice; whoops, of course I am."

"You're my first choice when it comes to castles."

"Well, I'll take what I can get. What's up?"

I told him about the evening and the wonderful introduction to Burns and asked if he knew the poem of the red rose. He laughed and said he did, but after hearing about Gordon's rendition, he wouldn't even attempt to recite it.

"You can't really tell me you can recite all four verses?"

"Now you're asking for it."

And he did. Not quite as rich a tone as Gordon, but his 'Southern' English dialect handled the Scot well and I couldn't believe I was so under educated.

"Perhaps your schools don't require as much literature as ours."

"Your high school students are equivalent to our college students."

"We call them secondary schools and some are government funded and others we call public are in fact more expensive and exclusive schools run by headmasters, and headmistresses, but all offer a top notch education."

"And why do I believe you went to Eton?"

Caught me."

We talked some more about the Carlisle Castle and, as I suspected, he had studied its architecture quite extensively. He wondered if I knew yet how long it would be before I reached Edinburgh and I assured him I'd give him heads up a week before I would arrive.

As our conversation came to an end, he said, "Fare Thee well awhile."

And I replied, "A knight and a poet, be still my heart."

Chapter Eight

That evening I had an unease of heart. My mind kept saying no, no, but my heart didn't seem in sync. After speaking with Sam I called James and tried to have him experience the enthusiasm I'd had with the rose poem and Robert Burns.

"He read the poem so well in Burn's original dialect."

"Well, after all he's a literature professor."

"Oh, I know, but I felt so under-educated."

"You teach history."

"Did you ever memorize a poem, or read the rose poem?"

"I'm a chemistry professor."

And so it went, my James, my love for the past ten years, so matter a fact, so content with his life and lifestyle. I wondered how we had been able to mix our interests together; they seemed so diverse. I questioned if my attraction to Sam had to do with our similar interests or a feeling I had discovered myself when I was with him. I needed to be careful and keep my head and shush my heart.

After a restless night with no dreams of ancestor, probably because of my real life issues, I hurried to catch the train to Durham. I'd missed my coffee and the trip from Northwest to Northeast England would only take a little over an hour so I didn't think I'd be able to get coffee aboard, but to my delight the dining car had coffee, tea and breads of all kinds. I loved these English breakfasts and grabbed my favorite scones, which lately seemed to be the sweet raisin variety.

This would be a trip without a castle destination as first choice. My paternal grandmother's name had been Durham and in our tree the name led back to a town named Pittington, just north of Durham. I wanted to go there and check for a Sir William Thorne Durham born in 1558, his son William in 1578 and his son Thomas in 1604. Thomas immigrated to Bermuda and his son Henry Thomas, born 1634 in Port Royal, later became Governor of Bermuda.

Before Sir William Thorne Durham, the surname becomes Thorne. Strangely the changing of names to that of location and other things is quite prevalent. The Thorne's came from Northampton, in central England, where George Washington's ancestors lived; couldn't find a connection to him, however.

Arriving in Durham on a nice sunny day around mid-morning, I found my reservation at the Kings Lodge Hotel and had lunch in their cozy bar. In visiting with the bartender, he said he had a friend who would transport me to Pittington and wait for me to search records all for a reasonable cost. He told me Rufus was a college student needing to work part time. Against my better judgments I said okay and within fifteen minutes a young man, probably around nineteen, arrived.

"Hi, my names Rufus Bell."

"Hi, Rufus. Are you ready to take me to Pittington?"

"At your service, ma'am."

"You can call me Leah."

He had a pile of unkempt straw colored hair and bright green eyes. His exuberant disposition lit up the room and I thought at least he's bright and clean and not a doper, by the looks of it.

In less than an hour, riding in a well-kept Ford Fiesta hatchback, we reached Pittington and I spent the next three or so hours diligently going through records at the courthouse with the aid of a very helpful white haired woman, named Esther, who said she had been working here for twenty-five years. She told me after checking city records I should also check country records in Durham, the county seat.

After due diligence I found Sir William Thorne Durham, and his sons listed in the pages of Pittington records and I confirmed the information in my mother's genealogy records. The only mention of occupation seemed to be 'estate', so I imagined them as somewhat well-to-do planters. It became a thrill each time I saw a Durham in the records. My mother had loved her Grandmother Durham; she told me how this short, stout lady seemed to be rooted in wisdom and common sense and how she had taught many a lesson at her kind knee and gave love in her warm hugs.

Feeling proud I'd located the Pittington relatives, I went out looking for my young driver. He had fallen asleep and looked even more ruffled, but had the same warm smile on his sleepy face. We visited on the way back to Durham, and I found out his father sat on the city council and lived in one of those grand looking Victorian townhouses. Rufus planned on going to London after he graduated in Business Finance, and become a wealthy financier. Oh, the optimism of youth.

That evening I ordered dinner to my room and spent the evening transposing my notes and watching the tele. I realized how good it felt not to be bombarded by the negative newscasts in the States. I loved that the commercials did not interrupt programing, but placed at the end, and the news seemed to cover more than just the many tragedies of the day.

I called James before bedtime and told him I'd be in Durham a day or so more and then head for the northwest border towns where many more skirmishes happened between my Scot and English ancestors over the years.

He said, "Who do you favor, the Scots or English?"

"I always felt the English were the bad guys and rooted for the Scots. I'll have to answer your question after I study more about the Scot kings, but I believe imperialist English king's encroachment into

Wales, Scotland and Ireland will still throw me into camp with my Scot ancestors."

"I hope you get the past put away and return to the future someday soon."

"Once I return after this year, I'd think I could put my ancestry away for good. But you have to remember I'm a history teacher and can't put history away any more than you can put your chemistry theories aside."

"Alright, maybe I'm only referring to your ancestral history."

"I understand how that might seem self-serving, but I think I understand history better by personalizing it."

We said our goodnights and he again warned me to be careful and stay safe. I thought he made sense, without his knowing why.

I sat up in bed, sipping a hot herbal tea, wondering if seeking the historical distance seemed safer than facing the uncertainties of the present or the future. I knew Mother felt her next reincarnation would be less traumatic. Of course incarnation meant a life totally different than her ancestral quest, but she also believed in Buddhist principles of karma and reincarnation. Mother, the escape artist; did I too exist in her world.

The next morning I visited the Durham Castle, located in magnificent grandeur, high up on a hill, with its cliffs impregnable by enemies; one of the few towns not captured by the Scots. It was not open for tours, as it held dormitories for Durham University students. After a pub lunch, I took a taxi to Lumley Castle, about a six miles distance, now a hotel, owned by Lord Scarborough. I had Scarborough's in my ancestry; John in 1520, followed by a William, three more Johns, all from the London area. The latter John immigrated to Pennsylvania sometime in mid-1700.

The hotel has fifty-nine rooms and is elegantly presented and is a back drop to Durham County Cricket Grounds. This old castle, originally home to family Lumley, has a ghost tale of its own. It seems two catholic priests threw Lady Lumley down a well for rejecting the catholic faith. They told Sir Ralph Lumley she had gone off to become a nun; now it seems Lady Lumley floats up from the well and haunts the castle (hotel).

In research that evening on my lap top, I learned the Earl of Scarborough was a title given to Richard Lumley, not a surname. Lord Scarborough served in Parliament and assumed the surname Saunderson, although his brothers remained Lumley's. One can get lost with name changes and perhaps the surname Scarborough of my ancestors had changed from time past too, but I found no connection to Hotel Lumley's Lord Scarborough.

I napped a while, cleaned up and took a taxi to Durham's Old Elvet area, crossing the River Wear on the Elvet Bridge to the opposite bank from the Cathedral. I had made dinner reservations at The Grill @ Gadds Townhouse located in an 18th century house, with lovely Victorian décor. Young Rufus Bell had advised it. Now that I sat alone at a well-dressed table on a fringed Victorian style chair, I rather wished I had asked him to join me, and laughing at myself to think the young Englishman would be comfortable sitting opposite someone so much older, and then to myself, "You are not so old at thirty-four."

I ordered a scallop appetizer with black pudding and asparagus puree with my Beefeater martini. The black pudding being sausage made from pig blood, oatmeal, onions and seasonings. The appetizer and martini was a perfect match. I seldom order red meat, but The Grill was known for its perfectly aged and tender beef, so I ordered a 6 oz. fillet cooked perfectly a medium rare. The hand cut chips were wonderful, the miniature vegetables slightly crisp and I accompanied it all with a French Burgundy. So much for my frugality I thought, but somehow I felt my anxieties soothed by the great food, drink and lovely décor.

I slept well that evening except for one brief, scary dream where I yelled for help, seemingly from the bottom of a deep well, where I paddled madly to keep my head above water. I woke up before

I drowned, and wondered what the dream was telling me; or did I know.

The next morning I grabbed a Continental breakfast at the hotel and decided to spend the day getting to know city Durham. It's a hilly city claiming to be built on the symbolic seven hills. The name Durham means hill on an island. In the 19th century Durham was described as ". . . a beautiful city situated on seven hills, in a beautiful winding of the river Wear, along the banks of which are pleasant walks, covered with woods and edged with lofty crags . . . ."

The River Wear flows north through the city and its meandering encloses the city center on three sides to form the Durham peninsula. In the center, I found Market Place, the main commercial and shopping area of the city, where I enjoyed people watching on a paved Market Square, with the busy activity of sellers, buyers and visitors. Throughout the hilly, many treed streets and lanes I admired the well-kept three and four storied Victorian townhouses, most with white trimmed paned windows, and I especially liked the old stone houses covered with ivy. I wondered in which one young Rufus lived.

It was lunch time and I found a Chapter's Tea House near the Elvet Bridge and enjoyed a wonderful Greek Salad with tea. I'm not an expert about bridge construction, but I loved these Romanesque bridges on the river, their reflection in the glassy water turning the bridge into large ovals.

After walking along a path in dense foliage along the river, I decided to walk up many old stone stairways to reach the famous Durham Cathedral, located high above River Wear, and faced by Castle Durham across the Palace Green. The Cathedral is said to be one of the grandest buildings in the world; the finest example of Norman architecture in the whole of Europe. It took 40 years to complete, and is now a UNESCO World Heritage site. The twin towers stand grandly looking down on the river, a photographer's dream shoot at all times of year. Tall and massive columns line the nave with arches between and looking up you see the ribbed vault of the roof. Saint Cuthbert's tomb lies in the Feretory; at one time an early Saint modeling Christian values. The large library contains one of the largest collections of early printed books in England. There are daily church services here with the Cathedral Choir singing daily, except Mondays.

The sun began to set before I reached the hotel and I decided to have dinner delivered to my room and spend a few hours transcribing notes and writing another chapter or two of my book. It had been a very fulfilling day and I felt Durham to be one of my favorite stops so far. I called Sam and left a message I would be in Edinburgh on Friday. In the morning I would catch a bus to Bamburgh, about 70 miles to the north in County Northumberland.

Chapter Nine

As the bus skirted Newcastle upon Tyne the next morning, I read that Robert, William the Conqueror's oldest son, built a castle at this location and named it New Castle. Over time it has become a large commercial center, said to be a modern, multi-cultural city of the 20th century, an attractive, spacious city full of gracious, classical buildings. Being a port city, its rapid industrialization became inevitable with exportation of goods and supplies around the globe.

Arriving in Bamburgh, I took a taxi to Victoria Hotel, where I had reservations. Located in the historical district, with views of the castle, and next to the Village Green, I felt instantly at home in this old brick Victorian. I entered the lovely en suite room, unpacked my bags, cleaned up a bit and headed down to the restaurant for lunch. I couldn't resist another plate of tasty English fish and chip, doused with malt vinegar, accompanied by glass of dark ale.

Since I had read Bamburgh was home to one of the finest castles in England, I decided to roam on by and see if I could get in on a tour. I knew the castle was an early fortress and later home to Kings of Northumbria, and later Henry II built the keep. By the early 1700's the castle stood in ruins and later with renovations became an infirmary and a place for shipwrecked sailors. In 1890, Lord Armstrong restored it and it's now open to the public during certain months of the year, offering rooms for receptions and the like. The magnificent castle sits high on an outcrop and overlooks the coast, sea and islands in the distance, and has been used for many films, such as, Ivanhoe (1952), El Cid (1961), Mary Queen of Scots (1972) and Elizabeth (1998).

The afternoon tour had just started and I joined about fifteen others with a hunky young guide. Upon entering the main tower, known as the keep, the rooms open to public view, included a series of reception rooms, each more magnificent than the last; dressed with paintings and tapestries, rare porcelain pieces and fine furniture. From here we went to the Kings Hall, the Cross Hall, the Bakehouse (kitchen) and then the Scullery (clean-up area) and Dungeons (Medieval prisons).

The Kings Hall and the Cross Hall, rebuilt by Lord Armstrong as the castle's centerpiece, are the location for many functions, such as receptions. The large keep halls have vaulted ceilings and flagstone floors and offer a fairytale atmosphere.

A pretty young lady, with pale skin and very dark hair flowing over her shoulders walking along side of me, said, "When I find my Prince, I want to have my wedding reception here."

I smiled and asked where she thought she might find her Prince.

"I live in London and maybe Prince Harry will find me."

"Maybe so."

She laughed and we walked along together. Then I began to notice the guide seemed to have eyes for this pale young lady; every time he finished an especially long spiel, I noticed he glanced towards her.

"What's your name?" I asked.

"Meg, short for Megan, but I just like to be called Meg, Megan McElroy."

"Meg, could your Prince be our nice looking guide?"

"Why, do you ask?"

"I think he has eyes for you."

She turned to look at him, as if to see him for the first time. As we continued the tour young Meg and hunky guide chatted, laughed and I could see a connection; perhaps I missed my calling as a matchmaker.

Bamburgh is the ancient capital of the Northumbria coast. The countryside here is described as hauntingly beautiful. The large castle dominates the landscape with cottages and houses clustered around a village green at the base of the outcrop where the castle stands with a view to the dunes, the sea and the islands of Christianity in the distance. I would check out a boat to one of these islands for tomorrow's venture. The village had many shops and I stopped at a pub for lunch. Standing at the bar with many other patrons, the bartender seemed to know in what order we had arrived, I ordered a pint of lager. English beer is served at cellar temperature, and they consider our beer to be too cold and over carbonated. I'm beginning to agree; flavors stand out better when not so cold.

The waiter then took my order of pork pie; I've begun liking it as much as the fish and chips, and I sat enjoying another noisy pub lunch. I think I might miss that more than anything when I return home.

"Hi," said a voice standing nearby my table.

I looked up to see Meg. "Well hello, would you like to join me?"

"Let me get my drink first, okay?"

"Sure, I'm not going anyplace."

Meg came with her pint and ordered fish and chips and we visited about our castle visit.

"Did you get to know the guide after the tour?"

"Yes, we've a date for this evening. He's a student at university in Newcastle and works here part time."

"What's his name?"

"Michael Day. Bamburgh is his native home; his parents live here; his father is a banker."

"He looks like a nice guy, hope you have fun together. Why are you visiting Bamburgh, other than the castle tour?"

"I came with my mother. She's in pharmaceutical sales and when I'm not in school, I travel along with her."

"Where do you go to school?"

"In London; I go to a performing arts school."

"What is your specialty?"

"I play concert piano."

This young lady had so much poise and natural beauty; I could see her there on stage, her dark hair falling down her back, her chiseled features and pale skin drawing attention to her loveliness, but not away from the sounds emitted from her long fingers on the keys. Megan McElroy would be a name to remember.

We said our goodbyes, and I decided to take a taxi to see the Lindisfarne Castle out on one of the Christianity Islands. I'd heard there was a causeway to the island available only at low tide. Lindisfarne, also the name of the island, has always been a sanctuary for spiritual pilgrims and those looking for peace and quiet, except for the sound of sea birds chatting over their enjoyment of prolific hunting grounds.

The village of ancient cottages is said to be tumbled together in narrow streets and squares. The picture that fascinated me the most, however, was the fishing boats lining the sands, which go out daily for lobster and crab.

In this spiritual world, the Lindisfarne Priory is perhaps the most haunting reminder of the holy men who occupied the island since the 600's, including Saint Cuthbert mentioned earlier in regard to the Durham Cathedral. Here the ruins of the Priory recall ancient days when the Vikings plundered the Priory and drove the monks from their homes. There is a museum here which tells the early story of the Priory and how it became a center for Christianity.

But it was Lindisfarne Castle, setting on a rock high above the sea, that caught me breathless. It was built originally by Henry

VIII in 1549, but later taken over by the Stuarts in 1715, and then returned quickly to the English and by the 19th century it lay in ruins. In 1901 Edward Hudson bought it from the crown and restored it to its present lavish interior, which includes a mixture of treasures, including furniture, tapestries and paintings. I loved the gardens and wonderful view across the sea.

I barely got back across the causeway before high tide would have required me to take a boat for the six mile crossing. Back at the Victoria Hotel, I showered and took a nap before cocktail hour and dinner at Mizen Head, an upscale hotel/restaurant which serves fresh fish provided by the local fishermen. The atmosphere did not disappoint and I was graciously seated along a wall, under a painting reminiscent of a Winslow Homer seascape, not too far from other guests. I ordered my now favorite gin martini and an appetizer of fresh mussels. As I sat sipping my drink, Megan and Michael strolled by; Meg saw me and stopped to say hello and introduce Michael, who said he remembered me on the tour. They looked so perfect together.

Following my appetizer I ordered a crab soup and then a California Chardonnay to go with a broiled seafood platter. For dessert I had a marmalade sponge, which delighted me so much, I made a note to attempt to replicate the sauce.

In the evening, full and satisfied, I decided to do some research in regard to the kings and queens in my ancestry, so I begin with William the Conqueror, known as The Duke of Normandy, and wife Matilda of Flanders and their nine children; Robert the oldest, William in middle, and Henry the youngest, along with Richard and five girls, I'll concentrate on the Duke, his wife and Henry, who became Henry I of England.

William was the only son of Robert I, Duke of Normandy, and his mistress Herleva. Upon becoming Duke at a very young age, he faced the fact of his illegitimate birth, but he was backed by Henry I, King of France (not Henry I of England). A description of William that seems to hold the most merit is he was burly and robust, strong with great stamina, a fighter and a horseman. In 1051, the childless King Edward of England chose William as his successor on the English throne. William was descended from Edward's uncle, Richard II, Duke of Normandy. At Edward's death there was opposition to his appointment of William and Harold was elected by the clergy and magnates of England to be king. Harold was crowned on 6 January 1066, but by mid-October William, Duke of Normandy, to become known as William the Conqueror, and his troop's invaded England. The battle between Harold and William's troops lasted a day with Harold being killed by an arrow to his eye. William marched on to London, where the clergy had appointed someone else as king, so for the time being William secured Dover, parts of Kent and Canterbury and his force captured Winchester, where the royal treasury was. It was all over by 1070, when William was crowned ceremonially on Easter at Winchester.

William stayed in Normandy for the most part after his coronation, but returned to England in 1075 because of revolts, and left Matilda in charge as Duchess of Normandy. He was devastated by her death in 1083. It is said he had been a good marriage and he had never been unfaithful.

William had troubles with his oldest son, Robert Curthose, over succession and William eventually promised him to be Duke of Normandy upon his death. William, the mid-son succeeded him as an unpopular King of England, but he died in a hunting accident, and Henry, the youngest, became King Henry I. William died in 1087 four years after Matilda.

Henry I, known as Henry I Beauclerc, born 1069, reigned as king from 1100 to 1135. He was a fair and just king and the best educated of previous kings. In 1100 Henry married Edith, the daughter of King Malcolm III of Scotland; upon their marriage she changed her Anglo-Saxon name Edith to the more Norman name of Matilda, as their marriage displeased Norman barons. During Henry I's reign his brother Robert Curthose continued a quest to dethrone him, but eventually Henry's troops defeated Robert in Normandy and Henry became not only King of England but also of Normandy. Matilda died in 1118 at the Palace of Westminster, and buried in Westminster Abby.

Henry's only son, William Adelin, died aboard the White Ship which hit a rock near Normandy in an English Channel crossing. Henry was heartbroken, and now without a male heir, he made his barons accept his daughter, Empress Matilda, married to Geoffrey Plantagenet, Count of Anjou, as his heir. However, upon his death his nephew Stephen of Blois claimed the throne, and the barons backed him. Empress Matilda opposed Stephen, which led to a long civil war called the Anarchy. The war was settled by Stephen announcing Matilda's son Henry Plantagenet as his heir.

One of Henry I's claims to fame, if you can call it that, is having the most illegitimate children born to a king; he had more than twenty, and they turned out to be political assets over time. Henry's description was of a medium height man, greater than small, his hair very black and set back on his forehead; his eyes mildly bright; his chest brawny; his body fleshy.

Deciding this was enough biography for the time being, I sipped some more herbal tea and spent a night of dreams in the company of kings and queens.

The next day I travelled to Chillingham, about 5 miles in distance, to visit the castle, now a privately owned hotel. I'd heard so many tales of the ghosts and wild white cattle roaming the park, I wanted to see this unusual designed castle with four corner towers and an inner courtyard for myself. It had been all but destroyed in early years, but by 1590 was renovated and the main entry moved to the front, for the coronation of King James VI of Scotland. Further renovations took place in the 20th century turning it into a comfortable, stately hotel with landscaped formal gardens, as it is today.

The castle's 600 acre parkland lies surrounded by the grandeur of the Cheviot Hills. It's said it has been the home of the Earls of Grey and their descendants since its inception in the 1200's; another name in my ancestry. To my delight the castle hotel was open for tour. The James I Drawing Room was named for the visit of the king in 1617; here you see the grand Elizabethan ceiling, noted for its ribs and pendants. In 1298 King Edward I visited and the room named for him is the oldest in the building. It has been restored with furnishings of the 13th century. The grand Great Hall has a flag stone floor, suits of armor, heads of deer, paintings of King Charles I, James II and others and a great long table where they say you can imagine Kings and Queens, Knights, Lords and Ladies gathered for feasting and merriment.

I passed on visiting the dungeon and the torture chambers where the ghosts reside. I understood you could see instruments like stretching racks, leg irons and other deadly devices; I instead spent time in the landscaped formal gardens, woodland and lake. I didn't see any of the woodland's famous wild white cattle, about 50 head, who have been inbreeding here for over 300 years; but I could see why they would be happy in this location; along with badger, deer and fox. The lakes are full of fish and friendly ducks quack their presence along with the croaking of bullfrogs hidden in the marsh grasses.

I decided to head back to Bambaugh for lunch at my favorite pub and then do a walk about enjoying the bracing air of the countryside. I thought about the things I needed to do before the morning when I would catch a bus to Edinburgh; I needed to change the card in my camera; I had taken over 400 shots since I arrived in England. That might not seem like many to an avid photographer, but I'm only interested in *the* shot—not many, pack my bags and reconfirm my hotel reservations at The George, a hotel close to Edinburgh Castle. I would call James and tell him of my plans and touch base with Sam. I felt excited to see Sam again; we would have so much to get caught up on.

I ordered room service for dinner and munched on a sandwich as I transcribed notes for the day. I called Sam first, as he was on my time, and James so much earlier.

"Hi, I'm leaving for Edinburgh in the morning."

"Great, I'll be there before you, as I'm flying out early tomorrow to catch a business meeting after lunch. Where are you staying?"

"I made reservations at The George."

"Great, our company apartment is close by. I know a restaurant I'd like to take you to. I'll call you after your arrival to make arrangements, if that's alright with you."

"Sounds good. Will be nice to see you again."

"You too."

I called James at 11 o'clock as we'd planned, but my call went to message and I quickly told him I'd be in Edinburgh tomorrow and where I had reservations and, "I love you, honey and I hope you're missing me terribly."

I wasn't sleepy, so I decided to write some more about English nobility before leaving the country of their origin. I left off at Henry II, the son of Henry I's daughter Empress Matilda.

Henry II, also known as Henry Curtmantel, or Henry Plantagenet, established the Plantagenet dynasty, named after his father Geoffrey Plantagenet who married his grandfather Henry I's daughter Matilda. He married Eleanor of Aquitaine, one of the wealthiest and most powerful women in Western Europe at that time. Over the years they had eight children and tension over inheritance began to prevail. Eventually Eleanor sided with her sons against Henry and France, Flanders and Scotland sided with her. Henry struggled to find land and power for his sons but tension always remained as to who would be his heir. It's said Henry II was an energetic and sometimes ruthless ruler in attempting to restore land and privilege of his grandfather, Henry I. He is described as good-looking, red haired, freckled, with a large head; had a short, stocky body, and bow legs from riding. He was infamous for his piercing stare, bullying and temper. Eleanor had great influence over Henry and she managed England for several years and later governed Aquitaine, but was in house arrest for a time after siding with her sons against Henry. This treatment of women seems prevalent in medieval times, or like with Henry VIII; off with their heads.

Henry II has been depicted in stories, plays and movies over the years; for one being the central figure in the 1966 play, *A Lion in Winter*. Some say he established many abiding laws for England and others believe he had not been a good king, probably due to too many familial problems. He had the largest royal court in Europe because of his wealth, and it is said he tried to maintain a sophisticated household, combining his love of hunting and drinking with literary discussion and courtly values. At his death Eleanor sided with Richard I, known as Richard the Lionhearted, a great uncle in my ancestry, who became king for the next ten years, before dying from an infected arrow wound. There were rumors that Richard was homosexual.

Richard I's reign was followed by Henry II's youngest son, John, who had always been Henry's favorite. King John, known as John Lackland, ruled England from 1199 until his death 17 years later. During his reign, England lost the Duchy of Normandy to King Phillip II of France. John is credited for the Magna Charta, a document which is believed to be the beginning of the constitution of the United Kingdom. He has been chronicled as an able administrator and general, but had personality flaws; pettiness, spitefulness and cruelty. His worst fault however was said to be his lustful lack of piety. While married to his first wife, Isabella of Angouleme, he had many mistresses and some of them married noblewomen, which was considered to be unacceptable. It is from one of these mistresses, Princess Joan, my great grandmother was conceived. Princess Joan married Prince of Wales Llewellyn, a story of which I covered during my visit to Wales.

King John, with wife Isabelle, was the father of Henry III, also a great grandfather through another line. Henry III and King John, perhaps due to the marriage of Joan to the Prince of Wales, supported the Prince and yet Henry III's son, who became King

Edward I, defeated the Princes of Wales and was the one who delivered Prince Llewellyn's head to be on view at the Tower of London.

Henry III, also known as Henry of Winchester, was the first to reign over 50 years. He married Eleanor of Provence and they had at least five children, one being Edward I, his heir. Supposedly they had a long and happy marriage. He is described as strong in physique and impulsive in action; a thickset man of great stature, middling in height, a narrow forehead and one half closed eye. He was involved in the constant revolt of the English barons and social discontent was prevalent; here is where the Robin Hood tales began. The description of these relatives keeps me pondering my genes!

Henry III's son, Edward I, reigned as king from 1272 to 1307. This great grandfather was known as Edward Longshanks and The Hammer of the Scots. He fought along with his father during the rebellion of the English barons. Later he fought for an outright war of conquest over Wales. It is said he was a tall man for the time, thus his nickname of Longshanks; his height and his temperamental nature made him an intimidating enemy. He held respect from his subjects by his embodiment of medieval ideals as a kingship, as a soldier, and an administrator. He married Eleanor of Castile and they had many children, including his heir, Edward II, who was born in the Welsh castle of Caernarfon, and became the first English Prince of Wales.

Edward II, the sixth Plantagenet king, was considered to be a failure; his reign marked with incompetence and military defeat. He fathered five children by two women, but was considered to be bi-sexual. He married Isabella of France, the sister to three French kings, probably in an attempt to unify England with France. The marriage was doomed to fail as Edward neglected her for other pursuits. He is described as a powerful looking man, like his father, but lacked drive and ambition, supposedly dominated by his father so lacked confidence in himself. Along with many other defeats and misjudgments, his forces were defeated allowing Scotland to separate from England. Queen Isabella later, hateful of Edward, had returned to France and formed an alliance with Frenchman Robert Mortimer in Paris to invade England. King Edward II eventually abdicated and his 14 year old son, Edward III, who, with his mother, Queen Isabella, at his side, ruled England. Edward II was imprisoned at Berkeley Prison, in Gloucestershire and believed murdered there by an agent of the Queen and Mortimer.

Following the death of his father, his son, after becoming of age, ordered the death of Mortimer for treason and though he spared his mother and gave her a generous allowance, he dismissed her from public service. Edward III, after the disastrous reign of his father, transformed the Kingdom of England into a great military force and saw vital improvements in legislation and government; in particular the evolution of parliament. In 1337 he announced himself King of France, which was the beginning of a 100 Year War; a war that went exceptionally well for England. He was born at Windsor Castle and often referred to as Edward of Windsor; he achieved unprecedented popularity during his long reign. It is noted he could be temperamental and impulsive and was well known for his clemency. He was devoted to his wife, Queen Phillipa, and he never saw opposition from his sons. He has been noted as the greatest general in English military history. In his later years he depended on his sons for military victories and after his death he was succeeded by his ten year old grandson, Richard II, whose father, the rightful heir, Edward the Black Prince, was terminally ill. Richard II became the last king of the House of Plantagenet and the last of my royal ancestors, to my knowledge. He was deposed by Henry IV, who imprisoned him and probably murdered him in 1400.

Totally exhausted from my research of ancestors, I slept feverishly; finding it difficult getting them out of my head.

Chapter Ten

The next morning, after grabbing a cup of coffee and my favorite raisin scone, I found the bus and soon was on my way to Scotland. The trip would take about two hours, and somehow I felt eager to start my Scotland ancestor search in spite of my exhaustion from the night before. I needed to refresh my thoughts as to what I wanted to visit and make a time line for doing so. During my travels, I also hoped to find the ideal winter location for finishing my castle book. In the meantime, I'd stay a couple nights in Edinburgh and let Sam give me his castle tour. I'd talked with James the night before and told him where I would be staying in Scotland. Once again his voice seemed distant, or perhaps just the same old James, so matter of fact.

I checked into The George Hotel in Edinburgh and feeling hunger pains went down to the café for lunch. The friendly wait staff's brogue was difficult for me to understand; I'd have to learn to listen carefully. Returning to my room, I decided to stretch out and rest and wait for a call from Sam. I'd been researching things to do and read some warnings about safety in this large city. I wanted to believe any big city has its dangerous areas and one has to be diligent about ones surroundings. I awakened to the sound of my phone ringing and heard the voice of Sam.

"You made it."

"Yes I did."

"I'll pick you up at seven o'clock, if that's okay with you."

"I'll meet you in the lobby."

I watched him enter the hotel, glance around looking for me, seeing me and with a smile heading in my direction. He looked so good I felt a bolt of emotion rush through my body; dressed in a perfect fit gray suit and red patterned tie, his wavy sandy hair curling slightly above his ears, his green eyes sparkling and friendly.

And then he reached for me, lightly kissed my cheek and said, "You look terrific."

With my heart beating a mile a minute, I smiled; he took my hand and led me speechless to a waiting black Mercedes. The touch of his hand brought another surge of emotion; what is this, I thought. He had a driver, so slipped over close to me in the back seat, took my hand again, and said, "You're awfully quiet my dear Guinevere."

"I'm just in shock over seeing you again looking so handsome, and then this elegant black steed, my knight."

"Only the best for my Princess."

We laughed at our same easy role playing, and I began to get my senses back and we chatted about my ventures and he told me about some of his own. He had been given a promotion to the executive offices and would be moving back to London and making trips to Edinburgh several times a months and even New York City ever so often. "You see you can't get away from me," he laughed.

"And who would want to." Our bantering went on until we reached the restaurant, a very upscale choice; thank God I'd brought along a black designer dress that stressed my teacher's budget.

The maître di located us at a lovely table, dressed in white and crystal, in a quiet corner next to a view of a small landscaped lake surrounded by miscellaneous fowl, including lovely peacocks. I had Sam order for me from the French menu. He said the restaurant reminded him of one of his favorite restaurants in Paris that had numbered their duck servings since the seventeenth century and provided a postcard with the serial number of the duck on it to the guest. Sam said the pressed duck here was equally as good, just no postcard.

Finishing up the delicious and lovely presented meal accompanied by a fine red Bordeaux, he once again reached for my hand (did he know how it affected me). "So you ready to dance all night?"

"Do you like to dance?"

"Well, in fact I do; not a great ballroom dancer, but I move around with some style, I think; how about you?"

"Born to dance and can follow backward in high heels."

"That's my girl."

As I sat quiet over my after dinner drink, he asked, "What's my Guinevere thinking?"

And then I knew he could integrate knight, scientist and executive into the same package, and I could incorporate his Guinevere, wife to James, writer and traveler as well.

"I was thinking we'd better get some rest for our big day at the castle tomorrow; and honestly, if I felt your arms around me, I'd be just too susceptible to your charms."

"Then I believe we should go dancing."

With a smile I replied, "I want to maintain our warm kinship; to step outside those boundaries puts our relationship in danger."

Or take it to a new level?"

"I want to be loyal to my marriage vows; even though I lust in my heart." I tried to keep smiling and not let the moment become too heavy.

He looked at me quietly for a while; his eyes absorbing my being. I felt totally out of control, but had to still my desires.

"It's going to be okay, Leah. I'll be there for you. You look so good to me and we've shared so much of ourselves, I want more. But I can control my desires and we can keep our relationship as companions looking at castles. Don't be afraid of our attraction to each other; it can sustain time and place."

"Oh, I hope so, Sam. I've missed you and want you in my life and know I'm being selfish."

Back at the hotel after a light good night kiss to my cheek, I couldn't sleep. My body still felt the surge of passion I'd experienced being with Sam. I knew I needed to think seriously about what I wanted with our relationship and what I expected in my marriage. James and I had always had a stable marriage, if not a passionate one. We both lived our lives without expectations from one another and found satisfaction in the areas we had in common; although they were few. I would ask him to take the time to visit me when I found the place I would stay on for a few months; we needed to be together to renew our vows and our marriage; had I put it in danger by taking this time away?

After a very restless night, I dressed for the day of longs walks through the great Castle Edinburgh. I didn't feel hungry, but ordered a bowl of oatmeal and added walnuts and raisins for stamina I'd need. As I sipped my coffee, I heard a familiar voice say a friendly good morning and turned to see Sam, causal in kakis and light blue golfers shirt, which made his green eyes look blue-green.

"Here I am, your trusty tour guide. Are you ready to go and look for your ancestors?"

"I'm ready."

"Which ones are we looking for today?"

"I'm looking for ghosts of some of the early kings beginning in the early 7th century." I hesitated and pulled out some notes from my purse. "I'm looking for Kenneth I, Constantine I, Donald II, Malcolm I, Kenneth II, Malcolm II, Duncan I, Malcolm III and his son King David I, and later, Robert I, the Bruce, Robert II and James I, III and IV. James II and V were uncles."

"Good god, you've found all these kings in your genealogy?"

"My mother did. I have the tree on my computer."

"This castle fortress would have been the location of early kings of Scotland, so you might see their ghosts. Remains found here date back to the late Bronze age, making it the longest continually lived in site in Scotland. Your King David built Saint Margaret Chapel, located in the castle, in honor of his mother who died in the castle in 1093."

"I'm so excited to make this visit. Thanks so much for taking me."

"You're welcome. I've visited the castle so many times over the years I'll take you through without joining a group. There are war museums and other places I doubt you'd be interested in, but the Royal Palace and Great Hall, plus St. Margaret's Chapel will introduce you to many a royalty in your ancestral tree."

The large imposing castle stood high on a rocky volcanic outcrop above the city, called Castle Rock, located west of Old Town and at the top of Royal Mile. We parked and walked in the gatehouse where I stopped to admire the statue of great grandfather Robert the Bruce. Sam had purchased tickets earlier, so we were free to meander around centuries old roadways that had transported artillery, past tourist shops selling mementos, rooms of war memorabilia and finally reached Saint Margaret Chapel, the oldest building in the castle, and one of the only 12th c. buildings surviving. It had been restored in the mid-eighteen hundreds. I was enthralled with its golden simplicity and elegance, and it is still used today for various religious ceremonies and weddings.

Next along the way we came to the Crown Square, a courtyard laid out by James III in the 15th century. The Royal Palace is to the east of the courtyard and comprises various royal apartments, now lavishly restored, and originally occupied by the Stewart monarchy; Robert II and III and then James I through V. On the ground floor is the King's Dining Room and a small room that gave birth to Mary Queen of Scot's son James VI, born in 1566, a beautiful painted ceiling was added in the sixteen hundreds. The Crown Room is on the first floor, where the coronation stone is kept, plus other items of royalty; the crown, the scepter and the sword of state.

The Great Hall, almost 100 feet long, had been completed by James IV and his Queen Margaret of Denmark in the sixteenth century. It's known for the original hammerbeam roof; in which, Sam told me, meant an open timber roof using short beams projecting from the wall. It is really an amazing sight; dark beams, golden decorative wood walls with red painted spaces above, paintings, and chandeliers casting their glow on everything. Sam said that over the years it had been used as a military hospital and barracks for the troops. It is currently used for various ceremonial occasions and a BBC program is broadcast from here. Adjacent to the Great Hall is Queen Ann Room, which used to be where the kitchen area was located. It is now a museum, and as I badly needed a sip of liquid, we decided I'd seen enough of my ancestors for the day, and returned to our car and stopped at a pub for lunch and drink.

"I need to get back to London and will catch a flight back this evening."

"Oh, Sam, so soon." He took my hand and told me our goodbyes made him sad and he would stay in touch.

And then I found myself back in my room and I cried. What was I to do? This was so not part of my sabbatical, not on the agenda, not anything I ever thought could happen to me. That evening the phone rang and his voice sent fireworks through my body once again.

"At airport and just wanted to say how much it meant to see you again. Remember to think of me once in a while."

"You know I will and thank you again for our time together."

"My pleasure."

And he was gone. But somehow my spirit was lifted. I thought if this is meant to be, so will it be, if not I've gained feelings I thought were dead and met someone so worth knowing.

Chapter Eleven

T he next morning I packed my bags, checked out of the hotel, caught a bus to my next stop in the city of Sterling; known as the gateway to the highlands. The city, originally a royal burgh of King David I in 1130, was the location of Sterling Castle located on a high bluff over the city; a castle acknowledged for the place of Scottish independence and a source of national pride. It is said the courts of many kings and queens provided a place of grandeur for visiting knights and people of influence.

We passed through Falkirk, located in a valley of the same name, in the central lowlands, a location known for the defeat of William Wallace by England's King Edward I. Dear Granddaddy Edward not only wanted Wales under English rule, he wanted Scotland as well.

Arriving in Sterling, I took a taxi to a B&B highly recommended by my guide book. I was pleased with the location close to the castle and my room spacious and comfortable and the main areas open, well furnished with great views out the many windows of the mountains in the distance. I'd spend a night here before taking a highland route to Iverness to visit Loch Ness and Urgquhart Castle.

The central village was within walking distance and I found a coffee house known for an excellent lunch menu and I wasn't disappointed with their potato and leek soup, scones and coffee. From here I was able to walk on up the hill to the castle. The castle's royal gardens offer an insight to the daily lives of occupants enjoying the small Queen Ann Garden for strolling amongst royal peacocks and to overlook the games below; like joisting tournaments. The expansive King's Knot, a formal garden, and King's Park, the royal hunting park, lay in the valley adjacent to the castle.

The James IV Great Hall, the largest banqueting hall ever built in Scotland, completed in 1503, is thought to have been built to impress his new queen, Margaret Tudor. The hall was also used to celebrate the baptism of Mary Queen of Scots' son James VI and later James VI celebrated his newborn Prince Henry here. It has also been used as a military barracks and depot. The restoration took 35 years with tons of stone for its grand exterior and oak trees to form the soaring high hammerbeam roof in the elegant interior with many fireplaces and two high windows to light the dais where the king and queen sat. Located close to the Great Hall are the Great Kitchens which prepared the food, brewed the ale and baked the breads.

Continuing on to the Great Palace, the palace of James V and his French wife Mary of Guise, I found one of the best preserved Renaissance buildings in Great Britain with an exterior of hundreds of sculptures. It is said James and his wife wanted to present themselves as wealthy, learned and sophisticated. The six main rooms are highly decorative in the Renaissance style; bright colors, expensive and ornate fabrics.

I decided to pass on the museum and went on to the Chapel Royal, the last building to be built at the castle by James VI in 1593 in time for the baptism of his first child, Prince Henry, who died at 18, before he could become king. The chapel was redecorated and a beautiful frieze and tromp l'oeil window painted by Scot artist Valentine Jenkin, in 1628.

Feeling somewhat exhausted after the long hilly climb and the castle tour, I went back to my room for a nap before getting dressed for dinner; but unable to sleep I decided to write some history of my ancestors I'd visited at the castle. First there was David I, who built the chapel in honor of his mother, Queen Saint Margaret. He was born 1084 and died 1153 and King of the Scots from 1121 to 1153. He was the young son of King Malcolm II and Margaret of Wessex and grandson of King Malcolm I. In 1115, Henry I, King of France, David's patron, arranged his marriage to Maud (Matilda), 2nd Countess of Huntingdon, allowing him to become Earl of Huntingdon. They named their first son Henry after the King. It is said David was a pious and fair man.

My next great grandfather was Robert the Bruce, otherwise known as Robert I, King of Scotland from 1306 until his death. He was born in 1274 and died in 1329. His parents were Robert de Brus, 6th Lord of Annandale and Marjorie, Countess of Carrick. Robert I became one of the greatest kings of Scotland, a fierce warrior and remembered as a national hero. He was the fourth great grandson of King David and led Scotland during its independence from England. His first marriage to Isabella of Mar produced one daughter, Marjorie, in my ancestral tree; he had four children with his second marriage to Elizabeth de Burgh and six illegitimate children by unknown women.

King Robert II, the son of Robert de Bruce's daughter Marjorie and her husband Walter Stewart, became king in 1316, the first monarch in the House of Stewarts. He married Elizabeth de Mure, my great grandmother, and had nine children. He later married Euphenia Ross having four children and causing later dispute over line of succession. Robert II's reign is noted for peace and prosperity.

King Robert III was the eldest son of Robert II and his wife Elizabeth Mure. His legal name was John, Earl of Carrick. He ascended to the throne at his father's death. He married Annabella Drummond; the story goes after she held him prisoner until he consented; now that's one feisty woman. Their son James became James I, King of Scotland following the death of his father.

Growing sleepy by all these ancestors, I decided to write about James I through James IV, kings belonging to the House of Stewart at a later date. Awaking an hour later, after dreams of warring hoards of knights battling each other, I showered and dressed for dinner. I had made reservations at a restaurant my hostess said was the best place to dine in Sterling, called a taxi and arrived at eight. In the taxi I thought about Sam and how I'd missed him today and now sitting alone even more. I just had to get back to being alone and feeling okay about it, as I had for most of my trip.

The friendly staff made up for the restaurants less than stylish décor in a large dining room with paned windows across the east and linen covered tables arranged along walls with a beverage bar in the center. I ordered scallops with a lemon thyme sauce and it was some of the best scallops I'd had on my trip so far. I sipped a glass of chardonnay with my dinner and had a nice sticky pudding accompanied by almond liquor for dessert. Returning to the B&B, I watched a little CNN, realizing I didn't miss all the politics, crime and mayhem, and then fell asleep.

At breakfast a lovely couple from Carlisle told me I should plan on a day trip to Doune Castle not far north of Sterling, so I checked a bus schedule, caught one to Doune and found a 14th century castle built by Robert Stewart, then Duke of Albany, son of King Robert II. It was planned as a courtyard castle, buildings on all sides of a large tower house. It is sited on the river Tieth at the confluence of the Ardoch Burn. From the courtyard you take stone steps leading to the restored Lord's Hall in the tower adjacent to the Great Hall. I made many notes in regard to construction as the pentagon shape of the castle seemed different than any other I'd seen. I wish Sam could have helped me understand what I was seeing. After a long day at the castle, I returned to Sterling and a nap before going back to the restaurant I'd enjoyed the night before. I ordered Salmon in dill sauce with baked vegetables and a couple glasses of Rose, forfeiting the dessert. Before I went to sleep, I translated the notes I'd made at the castle and decided to finish writing about the Stewart kings in my lineage.

King James I of Scotland (1394-1437) son of King Robert III, spent eighteen years as the uncrowned king in detention in England. He married Joan Beaufort and was finally crowned in 1424. He was known as a ruthless and acquisitive king.

King James III (1451-1488) married Margaret of Denmark and remained an unpopular and ineffective king, mostly because he did not administer justice fairly. He preferred music, hunting and riding to more war like behaviors.

King James IV, (1512-1547) the last king in Great Britain to be killed in battle, was a true renaissance Prince with an interest in natural and real science and was a good historian as well as musician who sang and played the lute. Well educated, average build, noble stature, handsome in complexion and shape, he was known as "King of the Commons", as he travelled around Scotland disguised as a common man. He married Henry II's daughter Margaret Tudor. His son James V followed him to the throne.

The next day I changed my mind again, instead of going directly to Inverness, I booked a four day coach tour of Scotland leaving Sterling around noon. I'd visited with people who recommended this tour and how it highlighted so many sights, offered good lodging and restaurants along the way that I decided to give up my independence for the company of others. After coffee and toast with marmalade, I packed, got a taxi and located the tour coach which had originated in Edinburgh, but stopped in Sterling. I boarded to find nine cheery travelers. I sat next to a friendly lady, Carol, who also travelled single and seemed glad for a like seat partner. Before we got to our first stop we had laughed and shared our travelling experiences and some of our personal information. She, probably about fifty-five, poised and attractive with a square jaw and striking gray eyes that matched her long hair loosely pulled back and clipped, had been widowed unexpectedly a couple years prior, and her children had arranged this trip for her to get acquainted with her land of birth which she had left as a child to grow up in Cincinnati.

Heading northwest over moorlands we passed several small towns until we reached the beauty of Glen Coe in one of Scotland's most scenic highland glens surrounded by mountains. It is home to one of Scotland's original ski areas. It is also a must do for mountaineers. Much of the glen is owned by the National Trust of Scotland. It is also the sight where the Campbell Clan annihilated the MacDonald Clan in the 1600's. The third Harry Potter film was also filmed in this area. We stopped for lunch at Fort William, located in the shadow of Ben Nevis, Britain's tallest mountain, a tourist destination with a beautiful setting on the banks of Loch Linnhe. After a pub lunch and a pint, feeling full and contented, we began our tour again, passing by many more lochs and mountains and arriving at the village of Invergarry where you enter the Great Glen, a valley that reaches east to west across the highlands. The Caledonian Canal was constructed here by connecting three lochs. The canal allows boats to travel from the North Sea to the Atlantic Ocean. We passed the Five Sisters, a range of five mountains and as evening approached, we travelled over the sea by a modern road bridge to Kyleakin for our stay on the Island of Skye, the inner Hebredes, for the next two nights.

Everyone was ready to get off the coach, stretch our legs and toss down a few pints, or the like. After whiskey cocktails at the bar furnished by our travel company to introduce us to the local beverage, we headed to our rooms, where we found our luggage, and had a chance to rest and cleanup for an hour before meeting again for dinner. I'd grown close to this flock of many colors: Canadians, Americans, a gay couple of guys from Australia, who kept us in stiches most of the time, a Japanese couple and Carol and myself. The restaurant was only about ten minutes' drive and we all joked we could enjoy our cocktails and not worry about driving. The management had prepared a lovely dinner for us and we feasted on brilliantly prepared and wonderfully seasoned salmon with whiskey sauce. After all this is the Isle of Scotch Whiskey and they featured it well, in cocktails for our arrival and aged single malt to toast our contentment at the end. We were pretty quiet, full and sleepy on our way back to the hotel.

The next day we traveled to see the Cuillin Hills, a vista considered to be unforgettable with dark vertical pinnacles of basalt, then on to the natural port town of Portree, meaning King's Port after King James V visit in 1540, with its village of pretty painted houses surrounding the harbor. From Portree we traveled to the ferry port of Uig, which ferried people to the Outer Hebrides, and then to Quiraing where we left the coach to walk through a landscape that dates from Jurassic times. We saw many sheep on our journey and the tour guide told us that after the Jacobite uprising and the defeat of Bonnie Prince Charlie, the clans were removed from the highlands and now its main resident were sheep.

Back in Kyleakin for the night we had free time to spend as we chose and Carol and I decided to try a restaurant we had heard of in the village of Portree overlooking the harbor. It was a short distance by taxi and the sparkling lights of the small village reflected in the harbor waters. We had a whiskey sour before each of us ordered a seafood platter. We realized the food from the sea could never be any fresher than here. We loved the small grilled lobsters, pan braised scallops and a wonderful stuffed and baked fish, served with miniature vegetables and accompanied by a very nice chardonnay.

Carol asked, "Are you glad you decided to travel by coach?"

"Yes, for sure. Before I left home I told my husband I wanted to go and see things on my own so I could take all the time I needed to explore. Now I realize the guided tour not only offers relaxation from driving, making reservations, and all, but allows you time to soak in all the sites."

"I agree and as I'm really not very adventurous on my own, it offers me a feeling of wellbeing I've lacked after my husband died. I do find, however, that the single supplement is somewhat onerous."

"I agree and with more and more single travelers you'd think they could devise a way to lower these costs for singles."

The next morning after a full breakfast of corn beef hash, poached eggs and toast, we started with a visit to the picturesque Eilean Donan Castle, situated on an island at the point where three lochs meet. When it came into view it took my breath away; an enormous medieval castle glistening pink in the sun surrounded by blue water. It is said to be the most visited and important attraction in Scotland. In early history it stood as a fortress, but in the 13th century it became a fortified castle and stood guard over the lands of Kintail (an area of mountains in the northwest highlands), the stronghold of the MacKenzie Clan. It has been rebuilt over the years and was all but destroyed during the Jacobite uprising in 1719. It remained in ruins until purchase by Lt. Colonel John MacRae Gilstrap and after twenty year toil it opened to the public in 1932. Supposedly Robert the Bruce wintered here in 1306 and 1307.

You enter the castle grounds by crossing a footbridge and begin the walk leading to the barred and studded front door into a foyer and then enter the large Great Hall. Here the stone walls, leaded Victorian windows, Douglas fir beams, a large fireplace and massive dining table dominate the room with its many large oil paintings on the walls and a beautiful tartan wool rug on the floor. The heart of the castle is its courtyard, which, with its many large rock formations resembles the shape of the island it sits on. The kitchen is the domestic heart of the castle and modernized in 1997, with an attempt to maintain the spirit of the kitchen and scullery. All the bedrooms are located on the third floor and here, once again, you see the very lovely tartan carpet.

I'd enjoyed the tour very much and getting to know another nice traveler, but I was ready to head out on my own to Inverness the next morning. After dinner with the new friends, we said our goodbyes, gave out business cards and the like and I retired to my room to pack, make some notes and give James a call.

"Hi, honey, glad I caught you at home."

"I'm not at home."

"Oh, well just glad I caught you because I wanted to tell you I'm off to hunt the loch ness monster in the morning."

"Tell me you haven't lost your mind."

"Well, I don't think so, but just joking you know."

"With your roaming about it's difficult to know."

"What's been going on with you?"

"Same old grind."

"Do you miss me?"

"Well, you're not here."

"Oh, James, sometimes your bluntness irritates me; can't you be a little less matter of fact?"

"You know how I am and I haven't changed."

"Ok, I'll call again in a few days. After Inverness, I'm going back down to spend a few days on the southwest coast of Ayrshire after a night in Glasgow."

"Is that where your Dad's paternal ancestor came from?"

"Yes, surprised you remembered. A Ninian McLain was born in Ballantrea in 1684."

"How could I not since you're obsessive about your ancestors."

"I suppose. From Glasgow I plan on heading for the east coast where I'll stay to write my book. Supposedly the weather is quite comfortable in the winter. Do you think you'll be able to get away?"

"Not sure."

With that we said good night and I didn't know whether to laugh or cry. You'd think I'd be used to James' flat persona by now, but perhaps I'd been so busy getting on with my life I hadn't had time to really think about it. Now, when I wanted an emotional connection it felt lacking.

Chapter Twelve

The bus trip to Inverness did not disappoint; how lovely these highlands so sparsely populated with many mountain ranges and lochs of all shapes and sizes. Inverness is the capital city of the Highlands and sits on the Ness River offering some of the most spectacular sights in Britain. I'd booked the Glenmoriston Town House, a hotel on the river bank. I found it very lovely and after a rest, I had lunch at a nearby cafe, and strolled through Old Town, with its Victorian Market, passed Inverness Castle, which is now the courthouse. I stopped at the Museum and Art Gallery and then returned to my room for a nap and to make reservations for evening dining at the restaurant located within the hotel; The Abstract, which had a Michelin rating, serving French style cooking using local ingredients.

I felt ready for a first class experience again and I wasn't disappointed. I started with a very dry Tanqueray martini, accompanied by Dressed West Coast Crab with Herb and Consommé Jellys and Tomato Sorbet. For the main I had the Pan Seared West Coast Halibut with Saffron Cocotte, Romanesco Puree, and Mustard Seed Sauce Vierge. The sommelier helped me chose a lovely white. After dinner I wandered into the piano bar, a dimly lit room, with sparkling lights and a lacquered black grand piano where a jazzman played my favorite swing sounds. I sat down, ordered single scotch malt on ice and as the darkness receded somewhat I saw my two gay friends from Australia at the same time they saw me.

"Please join us," said Max.

"I'd love to." And the waiter came and took my drink to their table.

How lucky for me to have found these fun guys; we drank, listened, and laughed for the next hour or two. I excused myself, finding it difficult to say good night, but I had a cruise on the River Ness starting early the next morning.

The blue and white cruise boat had about 20 tourists aboard for the two hour trip on the River Ness leading into Loch Ness and an hour visit to Urquhart Castle. We were greeted with a champagne cocktail and a brief history of the river and loch. Of course, the big question was when are we going to see Nessie the Loch Ness monster? We were told to keep our eye well peeled. It was a cool day in the autumn of the year requiring my jacket for the first time, but the air so clean you could savor the clear blue deep loch and refresh in its brilliance against the cloudless sky. I could have cruised all day and never tired, as I love being on the water, but without seeing Nellie yet, we stopped to visit the castle. The castle sat about two miles from where we docked at Dumnadrochit and we were transported by coach to the location. The castle is situated on a headland overlooking Loch Ness and originally became a fortress conquered by Edward I of England and then reconquered by Robert the Bruce. Later, Clan MacDonald and Clan Grant were constantly at war over its possession. It was partially destroyed during the Jocobite Uprising to prevent it falling in the hands of the Jocobites and subsequently decayed. It is now in control of the state. It is a magnificent ruin and one of the most visited sites in Scotland. It was one of my favorite days in Scotland, but sadly Nessie did not greet us.

I familiarized myself with the Jacobite Rebellion, which cumulated in 1745, and formed to restore the House of Stuart to the throne after Parliament's decision to dethrone King James II. The

King, a catholic, attempted to form tolerance with the Covenanters, protestant dissenters, but the Anglican Church was suspicious of catholic power and the Kings own daughters were Protestants. Eventually the Protestant Parliament, known as the "Immortal Seven", dethroned him. There were many uprisings over the years. The last uprising was led by William Edward Stuart, known as Bonnie Prince Edward, whose defeat ended the reign of the Stuarts. William of Orange, married to James II's daughter Mary, ascended to the throne. The name Jacobite comes from the Latin name for James.

I spent that night dining in my room so I could gather my notes and rest, and then another restful day and night before heading to Glasgow by bus. As James had indicated on the phone, this southern region of Scotland is where my father's early ancestors lived. My mother traced them from Northern Ireland to here dating back to the 17th century, with a few different spellings of their surname. I would search for them when I reached a village on the south west coast by the name of Ballantrae.

Locating a hotel with the name of Castle Hotel, immediately drove my decision to make reservations. How could I not stay in a castle? As I approached I saw the area landmark, which I had read about, a high square tower. Built in 1896, the rather decadent Victorian period, the contractor designed a baronial villa for himself. I loved it immediately and was greeted as a baroness arriving home. I reclined with the gift basket of fruit and sweets and read my guide book informing me that Glasgow is the largest city in Scotland. It is located on the River Clyde in the country's west central lowlands, and is an important financial center and is considered one of the best livable cities in the world. I thought perhaps I should reconsider the east coast for my winter stay; as this southern region has a warmer winter climate due to its location close to the Gulf Stream of the Atlantic Ocean. There is also the possibility of rainy, humid and gray skies in the summer similar to our Northwest States; that would not be on my desired list.

Being ready to hit the trail, I ordered a taxi which took me to town center, where I browsed the Gallery of Modern Arts housed in a 18th century neoclassical building. I feasted on my favorite abstract artists of the 1940's, some Impressionist works and found that Scotland had their own fine artists. I felt hungry so located a local pub for some pub grub and a pint. I will miss these eateries when time to go back home.

I decided to keep walking and stretch my legs and for the next couple hours I browsed the wonderful retail clothing areas where I found many designer shops (only looking). I passed Glasgow School of Art, one of the best I'm told, especially the library. The exterior and interior is considered a masterpiece laced with decorative detail, including the furniture exhibit within, all designed by Charles Rennie MacKentosh in 1896. I was lucky enough to arrive in time for a scheduled tour.

I walked a little further taking in the Glasgow City Chambers, an imposing structure of Victorian architecture inaugurated by Queen Victoria in 1888. I missed the tour, but was impressed by all the detail of the building and I understand the marble and the mosaics are very impressive. Although I have more of an interest in historical buildings, Glasgow is a very modern city of modern architecture. Among them the Clyde Auditorium with its great concrete curvatures and the Glasgow Transport Museum next to the tall ship on the river, the wonderful high-rise designed by architect David Chipperfield for the BBC headquarters, which is a focal point for the regenerated Pacific Quay on the banks of River Clyde along with the Glasgow Science Center, Imax Cinema and the Millennium Tower.

Returning to my hotel I made reservations in their lounge for dinner; a more casual location, but serving good food, so I heard. Arriving around seven all rested and ready for dinner, I was seated at a small table amongst the action, for which I am always grateful. I ordered a gin martini and an appetizer of small crab cakes in pastry shell. The lights were on the low side and a piano played in the background. I felt comfortable here. After dinner I popped by the lounge to enjoy the music. As I sat there sipping on the white wine I'd had for dinner, a waiter came by and brought another glass of wine, saying it was from a gentleman at the bar. I hesitated not knowing what to do. I looked over towards the bar and saw Sam. I could not believe my eyes.

"Were you thinking of turning down the drink?" he said strolling towards me.

"Oh, Sam, what a surprise."

He leaned down and kissed my cheek and asked if he could join me. I, of course, would not refuse him, ever.

"Why didn't you tell me you'd be in Glasgow?" He asked.

"Are you here on business?"

"Yes, it is a very important financial center for our company."

"Why are you at this hotel?"

"I stay in Glasgow at our executive suite downtown, but I love to come here in the evenings, never expecting to see you here." He ordered himself another drink, as I already had two before me and added, "I can guess why you chose to stay here."

"Yes, a castle is not to be refused."

We sat silently then just looking at each other. He had on a lovey navy suit with white shirt and burgundy patterned tie. He still let his dark blond hair grow just long enough to curl a bit at his ears. He looked as handsome as ever.

"So when did you get to the city?"

"Just this morning."

"Have you seen the town?"

"Much of it today; so lovely, a marvelous modern city with just enough history to make it interesting; have you been here long?"

"A couple days, will be leaving for London tomorrow. Where do you go next?"

"I'm going to Ballantrea on the southwest coast to look up some earlier ancestors; my father's paternal ancestors came from there."

"Where were you before Glasgow?"

"I took a tour coach from Sterling to Island Skye and the on to Inverness where I looked for Nellie and visited a castle."

"You've been busy and I've missed your calls."

"And I missed yours."

"I didn't want to shake up your life with my persistence."

"Oh, Sam, you only shake it up in a very wonderful way. I miss you."

"Then why don't I take the weekend off and we can drive along the rugged coast line to Ballantrae. We could drive over in my rental car and believe it or not I know a nice place to stay in that location. What you think?"

"It would have to be separate rooms."

"Of course. I know we are just great friends and only in the past were we more than that, dear Guinevere, and it sometimes seems to permeate our present. I'll be on my best behavior just to be with you again."

"I'll have to watch myself because you always look so darn handsome."

"Maybe that will work for me."

"Stop that."

As we sat talking quietly and enjoying our drinks and the music, Sam stood and offered his hand, "Let's join the dancers," he said. I looked at him for a minute, not moving, and then he took my hand and led me to the floor. With his arms around me we moved gracefully to the swing music. Being thus fully engaged I lent my body to him with ease and enjoyment, never wanting the music to end. What is that old song, *I could have danced all night* . . . . ?

"You feel as you belong with me," he whispered.

"Ummmmm," I responded.

The music stopped and he held my hand and said "See, it wasn't so bad."

"I never thought it would be. I think I said it might be dangerous."

"In what way? I didn't step on you did I?"

"Don't be silly."

When we said goodnight, he pushed my hair back from my face and gave me a light kiss on the lips and said he'd meet me at the restaurant for breakfast at seven-thirty. Attempting to sleep, my body remained alive and longing. Tomorrow with the music and dancing behind us, we can just be our fun loving, agreeable self's, I thought without a lot of conviction.

Chapter Thirteen

S am entered the restaurant in a pair of great fitting jeans and white shirt. Does he ever not just look awfully sexy, I thought. And just then he said, "Hey, you fit your jeans very well."

"So funny, I was thinking the same about you."

We sat, ordered coffee and then a light breakfast; made light talk about sleeping well (not) and our schedule for the day. His red convertible spoke of a fun day and we headed north out of Glasgow for a thirty mile drive to a small village by the name of Inverkip located on the upper Irish Sea coast of Ayrshire. My several times removed great grandfather, John MacLain, resided here in the mid 1600's. He is probably the grandfather of Ninian who lived in Ballantrae in South Ayrshire and according to probate records my mother had located, he was a merchant. I learned Ballantrae was an ancient fishing port, so couldn't help but wonder if these ancestors in my father's family tree, were of the sea, as Ninian's son William, born in Ballantrae, later moved to the east end of London where he met and married Rebecca. His move to this location could have been due to its proximity to the port of London, as their son, William, became a sailor on a slave ship and during his time at sea it is said he met and married an Irish lassie in Londonderry, North Ireland; another port of call. Mother could not locate the name of William's Irish wife, so this is not a fact but a possibility. They had a son named Benjamin, my eighth great grandfather, who immigrated to the United States from Atrim, Northern Ireland in 1796.

The village of Iverkip in the mid sixteen hundreds, the time of John's presence there, had the reputation as a place of witches. It seems Auld Dunrod, of the Dunrod Castle, the last of the Lindsay's, lost his mind and fell into the black arts. Rumors abound about how he was in league with the devil. Now, witches are long ago in history, and Kip Village is a marina development surrounded by many lovely homes and hundreds of moored boats with direct access to the waters of the Firth of Clyde, a large body of water protected from the Atlantic at the top of the Irish Sea. Since it is only a thirty minute drive from Glasgow and offers unspoiled coastline, islands, harbors and villages along Scotland's west coast, it is a very popular location for sailors and other visitors.

I loved this coastal route where the water was warmed by the Gulf Stream current and the shoreline glistening with waves breaking against its craggy rocks. It had been a day where Sam could keep the top down on the convertible, and I felt the rush of wellbeing as the sea mist met my lungs. We travelled through the lands of Bruce and earlier kings, where my later ancestors also lived, which offered a different perspective than those ancestors of medieval times.

We stopped in Ayr for lunch and found a café offering lamb stew and fresh baked bread, which we accompanied with dark ale. During lunch Sam told me about the castle he wanted to visit next. "It's now a ruin, but many ghosts are there of your ancestors, like very early medieval kings when earlier castles stood in the same location. The third castle, the one we will visit, was built in 1371 for Robert II, who followed his father, Robert the Bruce as king of Scotland."

"I'm so lucky to have met up with you on my travels. Thank you so much for your help in my understanding of ancestors and castles."

"It's been my pleasure, Leah."

After lunch we drove a few miles south of town and sitting on a high hill overlooking a panoramic view of the Ayrshire countryside, which has had human occupation for over 4000 years, stood the remains of a once magnificent Dundonal Castle. With its coastal backdrop, origins of the Stuart dynasty and home of kings for over 150 years it reeked of history. We parked below and walked the 140 feet up to the castle, coming to what used to be the outer courtyard used for the stables, blacksmiths and brew house and is now a grassy courtyard. We then entered the inner courtyard, where Sam pointed out the remains of a Chapel dedicated to Saint Ninian.

"I'd not heard this name before seeing it as the first name of my early ancestor, and thinking it a very odd name. I need to research Saint Ninian."

"I've read some things about him, but mostly know there are many sights in Scotland and other places dedicated to him and there is no historical evidence that has been uncovered about him, only many myths of his existence.

"I wonder if my great grandfather was named for that Saint; his son also named his eldest child Ninian."

"I really have no idea how common the name is, this is my first encounter with it, but it sure seems a possibility."

We entered the lower floor for use by the servants and more storage, and then upstairs to the main floor to the Laigh Hall, a large banquet hall, and finally the third floor where the Great Hall resided. Going back down we walked along the outside wall where five shields are located, which belonged to Robert and his family for heraldic pursuits. You can also see the remains of earlier castles here and where a loch was formed for fortification and also to provide fish for eating.

"Are you in for a walk along a path leading to one of the many royal homes located in this area in earlier times?"

I assured him I would love to and we headed across a bridge towards the ruins of the Aachen's House, important aristocrats of that period. The path led us on a delightful stroll through flora and fauna among ancient woods. You could see the ruins had been an elegant mansion in its time, located in a lovely nook in the woods close to the castle.

Back in the car we both thought the location here on the Ayrshire southwest coast one of the prettiest you could find anywhere. I leaned back and with the gentle breeze in my face, I wordlessly took in the moment; great companionship, lovely views, and the peacefulness that I always felt when near the sea.

We drove to a small white cottage, close to the village of Ballantrae, and located close to a well-known golf course. "We're here," he said, "This cottage is owned by my company to provide a get-away for those visitors or employees wanting to golf or just to visit this beautiful coastline in Rabbie Burn's country."

"It's lovely, I love the yellow shutters and cottage garden."

"If you decide you like this location for your winter stay, I might be able to locate a cottage similar to this that would be available. There are several for rent during the winter months."

"It's a possibility. After I visit Aberdeen and travel the eastern shoreline, I'll get a better idea of where I'll receive the most inspiration for writing."

"You'll find it quite a bit more expensive on the eastern shore, and winter is colder than on the southwest coast located closer to the Gulf Stream. However, you may like the weather better on the east coast, although it is colder, it isn't as rainy."

"I guess with the ever changing weather patterns around the world, we expect what is unexpected; global warming and all that."

"Yes, it's beginning to look that way."

Entering the cottage, I exclaimed at the openness of its rooms; a large great room effect with stainless appliances in an all-white kitchen nestled in a corner with a granite topped counter with four stools, a large fireplace and wall bar in the living room with wheat colored stuffed sofas and blue chairs, a large glass and brass coffee table and occasional tables. The French doors facing southwest overlooked the blue waters of the Irish Sea in the distance. Two bedrooms with en suite bathrooms were located on opposite sides. My room had a queen bed dressed in a deep blue comforter with nautical design on the many colored pillows, blue and white shell papers in the bathroom, white stained rough cedar walls and old wide planks of pine covered the floor, as in the rest of the cottage. The windows, lined in sheer white drapes, looked out across the countryside with a view of the golf course winding around knolls and sandy dunes. There were blackout shades for night time or privacy.

"Let's have a drink on the deck and then I made reservations at eight for dinner. I think you'll love one of the best food places I know of."

We sat on the deck overlooking the valley with the sea in the background. The evening was cool and so quiet it seemed you could hear the waves come ashore. The valley below stretched its green and gold splendor across the landscape with dots of white cottages topped by red roofs, animals large and small grazing on the plentiful grass, country lanes with passenger cars and farmer's trucks looking as miniatures in a small boys collection and out on the blue sea the white sails of boats catching the wind.

"I keep thinking I will not find another site as perfect as the one before, and here I see unbelievable beauty again."

"Yes, there is no wonder Rabbie Burns found inspiration here. It's one of my favorite spots and I'm glad we could share it together." He reached over to click glasses and added, "Let's be ready in about thirty minutes that okay with you? We don't need anything but somewhat casual and sweaters."

"Great, I'll change to slacks and sweater and be ready momentarily."

We drove along the winding road around the golf course and over a small ridge to the Cosses Country House near the village of Ballantrae. Sam said the Inn was popular for golf course members, but locals and tourists came here, not only for the food, but for the lovely views. We ordered a nice white Bordeaux to go with our appetizer of Ballantrae Prawns with Marlbra Smoked Salmon and for the main a nice red Bordeaux with Crailoch Lamb accompanied with garden vegetables and corgettes in garlic and lime, popular in Provence. Following up we had a fine old port with Scottish cheeses.

"And was I right, best food ever?"

"Absolutely, so fresh and perfectly seasoned, I relished every bite." Looking out the large window facing the sea I saw what looked like a large rock out a ways in the water and asked Sam about it.

"It's called Alisa Craig, a volcanic plug of an old volcano. It is formed by blue hued granite which for many years they quarried to make curling balls. It is now a bird sanctuary."

I also asked him about Burns, where he was born and died. "He was born in the village Alloway about two miles south of Ayr on the river Doon. His father was a gardener and the family was poor and Burns worked hard as a laborer for all of his early years. When he was twenty-nine, he moved to farm near Dumfries and died in his thirty-seventh year, in 1796 I think."

"Did he ever marry?"

"Yes, it seems he had several children with servants of others, and then got a girl pregnant who later delivered twins. Her father sent her away and disliked Burns. Later, when Burns moved to Dumfries they reunited and married, having a number of children together, though it's rumored he still had an eye for the women."

"I guess his romantic poetry was formed by his many liaisons. But none the less I'll always love his Red, Red Rose."

"I remember you had me recite that once."

"Yes, after I heard a literature professor recite it on one of my journeys. I still think Great Britain, has a far better education system than we in the states."

"Perhaps, but you spent a couple hundred years developing a new country begun by only a few discontented souls who managed to hang on through adversity to form a country that became the leader of all nations; much to our chagrin."

"Well a leader in some ways."

Sam took my arm to lead me out the front door and then found my hand and we strolled to the car. On the way to the cottage I asked if he would mind me not going back to Glasgow with him, but catching a bus and going to Dumfries. He said he'd miss my presence, but he realized I would have to backtrack if I accompanied him. We had a nightcap at the cottage bar and then I quickly gave him a hug and said goodnight. He stood there quietly, I felt his gaze follow me as I left the room. I knew I had to reach the room and close the door in order to prevent something I wanted very much, or at least my body did. It was a restless night and I had to resist the temptation to go to him. I knew I was in trouble and would have to figure out what to do about it. I hadn't talked with James for a couple days and the last time he still seemed unsure whether he would join me during the winter months. Maybe it is time to return, I thought.

The next morning Sam wanted to take me for brunch at a close by castle. The Glenapp Castle was famous for tea and its magnificent gardens. He told me it was his second choice for dinner and wished we had another day for me to compare it. We talked easily over our food as if we were comfortable about everything, but I knew we both were hiding behind our true feelings. He took me to the bus depot in Ballantrae where I purchased a ticket to Dumfries.

"Sam you know I hate leaving you but also you must realize you are such a temptation for me. I feel I lead you on and then turn my back on you and I can't allow myself to do this to you."

"Leah, please, it's okay. I respect how you feel and choose to be with you. Of course, I want more and I suspect you do too, but let's not ruin what we have by overstepping your principles. We have time to sort this out. I want to see you again and don't worry about me, being with you is enough for now."

We hugged tightly, I loved the feel of his arms around me, and I stepped on the bus.

Chapter Fourteen

I spent the two hour trip to Dumfries trying to clear my mind. I couldn't remember in my life having such a strong attraction to anyone. Perhaps it had to do with my many years of career building and a husband dedicated to his own profession, with less thought of personal needs. For the past year James had been mentoring PhD candidates and he loved it. I knew James had his hands full and had never been one to show his feelings. At times I thought he might have some problem with expression of emotions, but he was steady, honest and hardworking, what else could you want in a man? I asked myself. And I knew the answer when I thought of Sam.

The B&B where I had made reservation was beyond charming, right out of a Robert Burn's poem with red roses everywhere. I rested in the very comfortable bed for a while, sipping on a pot of hot tea provided in my room and reading my guide book. I would pull myself together and get on with my agenda. Sam was a distraction and that was all; I tried to convince myself.

I remember I never visited Key West, Florida without thinking about Hemingway, visiting his home and having drinks where he did. I loved his cats roaming all over the estate, many of them with six toes because of years of inbreeding. Now in Dumfries everything reminded me of Robert Burns, so I decided to have lunch at the

Old Globe Inn where he was known to imbibe. It is a wonderful old inn, all dark woods and sparkle of light from many globes. I had a dark beer with a Rueben type sandwich. From here I caught a taxi and drove to see Ellisland Farm where Burns had lived. It was late autumn and all the lovely trees were changing colors. The farm, with all white buildings glowing in the distance, is where Burns penned some of his more famous poems. I enjoyed this popular visitors site as a guide walked us through the house and out to the stables.

As I arrived back to my residence, I stopped by the large, comfortable living room where afternoon tea or wine with small sandwiches and condiments greeted guests. I sat on a divan and visited with a couple from London. I mentioned my friend Sam and they knew of the family and said they were considered a prominent family, both for Mr. Adam's architectural achievements and their generosity to worthwhile causes. They said their son also was known for his achievements, especially in technology research.

I rested for a while in my room before showering and dressing for dinner reservations at Bruno's where Sam said had fresh homemade pasta and other traditional Tuscan dishes. I was feeling somewhat melancholy and would have liked to have curled up in the comfy bed, but time and awareness had taught me when I felt this way the best remedy was to get out with people, even if I just sat amongst them. I started out with an aperitif of Dubonnet and soda and Insalata Caprese, a dish of fresh mozzarella cheese and tomatoes garnished with fresh basil, olive oil and cracked pepper. For my main I ordered Spaghetti Marinara a dish with mixed seafood, garlic and tomatoes and a touch of chilli spice, accompanied with a couple glasses of dry rose. I felt comfortable in the Mediterranean atmosphere influenced by the owners Tuscany upbringing. Passing on dessert, I decided to walk the short distance back to the B&B. I felt safe in this well-lit historic district and I needed to move around more.

The next morning after a breakfast where I enjoyed very tender crepes filled with fall berries and a glass of champagne, I met a tour which would take me to visit Caerlaverock Castle south of Dumfries. The ruin still very imposing with its triangular shape surrounded by a large water filled mote was home of Clan Maxwell from the twelfth century and is now a Scottish Heritage site. We toured what remained of many rooms and walked along the nature trails of the adjoining reserve. I felt invigorated from the fresh air, exercise and friendly tour bus passengers. Although this was not a place where ancient ancestors lived, I felt the presence of my Bruce ancestors in this part of Scotland and learned King Alexander II, gave this location to the Maxwell's to build their castle and I do have him in my tree.

That evening dressing in my loungers, the staff graciously furnished me with a nice pot of chicken soup, home baked saltines and hot tea with honey. I responded to some emails and typed some notes in regard to structure of triangular castles I'd received from Sam before I left Ballantrae. I thought of calling James about my flight to Aberdeen in the morning, but decided I'd wait until I got there and check out what my itinerary would be going on down the eastern seashore to find a place to write for the winter.

After good-byes and thank you to my hosts and farewell to other friendly people at the breakfast table, I got a ride in a small transport van back to the airport in Glasgow. As the plane taxied down the runway and up over the scene below, I felt a twinge of goodbye—I would miss this Southwest region of Scotland. Maybe I would come back here to write. Was it the voice of my ancestors calling to me?

It was a rainy day and our flight ran into some turbulence, but we landed in Aberdeen close to schedule. I had read that in the rain Aberdeen's granite structures gleamed and sparkled in the sunlight. I felt privileged to see this for myself. I got a taxi to my hotel, the Skene Hotel at Whitehall, an apartment hotel, in the central area of Aberdeen. I could walk to galleries, the theatre, restaurants and even the beach. Since there were at least four castles I wanted to visit near Aberdeen, I would be here for at least five days and I wanted a well located hotel. The staff were friendly and alert to making their guest comfortable. The structure was a traditional Edwardian storied construction of granite with ornate features. I'd booked a one bedroom suite because I decided to spend more nights in my own kitchen instead of dining out, as I had a lot of notes to transcribe and knew I would have more after the castles I would visit in the area.

After unpacking I wandered around central Aberdeen and felt it lived up to its reputation of a city known as "The Flower of Scotland" with all its lovely parks and gardens. I walked by museums, the theatre and art galleries in this Granite City and would take time later to visit. I'd especially like to attend theatre one evening, it had been a long time and I was ready for some culture, other than my ancestors and castles. As I had missed lunch, I stopped by a small pub and had a glass of beer with a pork pie.

Back in my room I put on comfy p.j.'s, took a little nap and then worked on my notes for a while. I decided this first evening I'd eat at Bistro Verde, a restaurant I'd seen on my walk about. Tomorrow I'd find a grocery store and pick up a few easy to prepare items, include some wine and nibbles. I showered and put on my dress slacks and sweater over tee and walked to the restaurant where I was greeted by a friendly hostess and seated at a well located table. I was hungry after my day of travel and walk and the menu had many tempting items. I ordered Dubonnet with soda and lime again for a light aperitif and a starter of scallops. For the entree I ordered a Thai Seafood with Curry and a glass of Gewurztraminer from Alsace in France, which I'd always liked to pair with curry dishes. The soft music in the background soothed me and I felt light in spirit on my return to the hotel.

Sometimes it seems when we feel all is right in the world, we're calm and assured, something is sure to come along to stir us out of our complacency. And then it struck that evening. Before I had a chance to call James I received one from him.

"So glad you called."

"Where are you now?"

"I arrived in Aberdeen around noon today."

"Were you going to call?"

"I actually just walked into my room with that on my mind, is everything okay? You sound stressed."

"I've decided it's time we had a serious discussion."

"What about?"

"I want a divorce."

I felt as if he had struck a blow in my solar plexus. I was numb struck, couldn't respond and took the phone and sat in a chair.

He continued, "I guess this was a poor way or a wrong time to say this, but I knew you wanted me to visit you soon, and you needed to know that is not going to happen."

I attempted to speak and found my voice barely audible, "Why?"

"Why I want a divorce?"

"What else," I croaked.

"It's a long story, but I've been seeing someone else since you left."

"Since I left, or before I left?"

"Well, both perhaps."

"Perhaps?"

"I've grown close to one of the PhD candidates."

"How close?"

"Well she comes over here or I go to her place almost every weekend."

"Isn't that considered misconduct for a professor?"

"I am not her mentor."

"But you are married."

"And that is why I want a divorce."

I didn't respond. I didn't have a response, it all seemed so impossible that quiet, conventional James could be saying these things to me. He remained silent at his end too, and finally I said, "Let me absorb all this and I'll call you tomorrow," and I hung up.

To say I was stunned would be an understatement. The disbelief disallowed his message to fully develop but suddenly I burst out in sobs.

After recovering enough composure to review the conversation I wondered if my distress was not only James' words, but my own guilty feelings about Sam. In my heart did I too want a divorce? I believe at the time I had pushed that idea far into the back of my mind. My traditional views were that marriage was forever, when difficulties arise you work through them and rekindle the love you had at the beginning. I truly believed this, but then I thought how James and I had never had a very affectionate relationship—maybe more of one that resembled a partnership for our career goals. I helped him get through his master's and PhD years, and then he helped me. Once we began our individual careers we seemed to have gone our own directions, intentionally or not, we kept separate bank accounts, separate investments, we never bought a house and only the necessary possessions.

I tossed and turned and couldn't sleep—got up a few times and wandered around the apartment thinking this hotel apartment had as much hominess as the one we'd lived in for the past ten years. Why hadn't we truly nested as couples usually do, why had we grown apart without even realizing it. Why didn't I ask him to give it time, to not just throw away our years together—was it I knew it was over even before he called? Had I suspected his infidelity even months before I left for the UK?

I'd tell him tomorrow to put my things in the guest room and I would have a moving company come by, pack them up and send them to storage. I'd tell him to keep the furnishings—I didn't want anything except what I had before I married him; some photos and keepsakes. My clothing could just be transferred to the other closet and he could add a few personal items and my jewelry, which I intentionally left behind, not liking to travel with anything expensive.

My car could also be transported when I knew where I would be living, or maybe I could drive it myself depending on my location.

And with that thought I realized I needed to get back to work. This sabbatical was for publishing requirements and now I would be on my own and although I had been a regular saver with a fairly large investment portfolio, my salary as a professor is what would be needed to support myself. James and I had always kept separate accounts, but we did share our expenses. That would end. I knew I didn't want to return to teach where we had lived and see James every day. I just couldn't do that. I would start a search for a professorship at another university. I wondered if Glasgow University might be interested and I knew The University of Edinburgh was highly regarded. I also thought about London University, and if all failed there were several universities I knew would be interested in my credentials in the States.

Two years ago I had received a fellowship in Digital Educational Research. I knew research was an area that many universities were short of professors to fill, and felt it would tie in brilliantly with my doctorate in History and my interest in historical research in the digital age.

Thinking of the possibility of applying in London brought Sam to mind. I wanted to call him to receive some reassurance and warmth from his words. I knew he would be a good reference for work in the UK, and might be able to help me decide on the best place to teach. But then I didn't want to entangle him in my troubles. Maybe later after I'd resolved some of my problems I would feel better about calling him.

I finally slept for a few hours and when I awoke I felt more in control of my situation. Instead of visiting more castles, except perhaps one or two to give me more notes to publish at least 350 pages of work, I would begin the process of finding a job. I ordered room service for some scones and fruit to go with the pot of coffee I made and sat down to work on my resume and get telephone numbers to call for an appointment back in Glasgow, Edinburgh and maybe London. Or if necessary other universities in the States. I'm not sure why I seemed to be preferring living in the UK. Maybe since my mom died three years earlier, I just wanted to find a new life among the ancestors she so endearingly researched.

I also needed to contact my office and offer my resignation as of the spring semester, as they would have to find my replacement. I really wanted to find a position before I resigned however. My mind was running a mile a minute. I needed to make lists to keep me on track.

Later that evening I called James and told him about storing my goods and car and that I would sign any divorce papers. I said I was sorry our years together were so easily discarded, but I wished him happiness. He seemed fairly unresponsive and said when he got the papers he'd need to know where to send them.

And so it was over. In a way I felt a sense of freedom and tried not to feel guilty about it.

Chapter Fifteen

I made an appointment for an interview at the University of Edinburgh department of history for the next day. I realized it was the top research university in the UK, offering me the best in my profession and the city offered more cultural activities for my personal life than Glasgow. My interview with Dr. Hammond went well, he seemed to be impressed with my work at a top ten University in the States and my body of scholarship, especially in research. He said they were presently looking for a history professor who could also head their digital history research program. He said they were working on a short time schedule to fill the position and he would let me know when to return for more interviews. I assured him I was interested.

The campus extended over a large area and I was impressed with the architecture and beautiful gardens close to the water inlet from the Atlantic. I felt I would be at home here and thought how wonderful if this would be my new life. I stopped by a familiar pub and had lunch. The beer hit the spot as I realized I was more stressed than I thought. Too much happening too soon.

I caught the bus back to Aberdeen to await, hopefully, for another call from Dr. Hammond. This was my third day in Aberdeen and I had managed to go to the market and pick up a few items: rotisserie chicken, fresh veggies and fruit and some lovely cheeses to go with the six pack of mixed red and white wines. For breakfast I found a package of my favorite raisin scones and some fresh ground coffee.

Back at the apartment I made arrangements to tour the Crathes Castle about 15 miles from Aberdeen the next day. I spent the day lounging around, sipping some wine, transcribing notes and checking my list. The noise of my phone's ring sound startled my silence.

"Hello."

"It's me, Leah."

"Sam."

"That's me. Somehow I felt the need to contact you. How are you and where are you?"

"I'm in Aberdeen, been here about three days."

"And . . ."

"How am I? Well that's debatable, but think I'm fine."

"Great, I'm glad you think so anyway. I'm going to be in Edinburgh tomorrow and wonder if you need any help viewing the many castles around Aberdeen, I could spend the weekend."

"I've made arrangements to join a tour to Crathes Castle tomorrow, but no plans after that. I'd love to see you this weekend, as a matter of fact."

"Our company has accommodations in Aberdeen. Where are you staying?"

"I have a one bedroom hotel apartment at the Skene at Whitehall, as I planned on spending a week or so here before journeying on down the coast."

"The Whitehall is a popular place. I'll call you around six Friday evening, and we'll have dinner at one of my favorites, if that's okay with you."

"Sounds wonderful, Sam. Can't wait to see you, have lots of happenings to share with you."

"Want to share a little now?"

"Ha. Always trying to get ahead of the game. Be patient my fine friend."

"Oh, right. Friend. Well this friend will see you Friday evening."

The warm, modulated tone of Sam's voice always soothed me. The combination of his father's North American accent with his mother's upper class English accent gave him a distinctive sound and then his added friendliness mixed with humor made him a lovely speaker. I knew why he spoke for his company at many events—he had ability and charm mixed in with humility. Oh my, I thought, don't start idealizing this man as that usually leads to disappointment

I rested well that night and thought my life could start anew without too much guilt about my past—no, without guilt. I'd always done my best and that was as good as I could do. I thought back to my mother's death and missed her very much. She was a positive influence in my life even though hers had been a difficult one. Mother grew up in a middle class religious family where faith and education were important. When she married my father, an atheist, and dropped out of the university to help him graduate, they were disappointed and disinherited her. I never knew them. I was born the year my father graduated from journalism school and accepted a position overseas and after a three year absence he asked for a divorce and my mother granted him one. He is now an international journalist of some repute, but I do not have a close relationship with him, although he calls some times when he is in town.

I've never known a kinder more thoughtful person than my mother. She went about getting a job and taking care of me to her best ability. She hadn't the education she'd aspired to, so along with raising me and working, she continue to take classes and finally received a degree in her fifties. She never had a lot of money, but somehow she seemed to make the most of it, saving for my education at the best universities and still taking time for herself. She worked at her administrative position with an accounting firm for 20 years and got an accountant position after receiving her degree. Four years ago she got a diagnosis of pancreatic cancer, which killed her within the year. She was even courageous in death—much more than me—I would miss her too much.

The next morning while I was reading my emails over coffee, the phone rang and Dr. Hammond asked if I could come by that afternoon around two o'clock and meet some of the other faculty members.

It would take about two hours to drive the 92 miles, allowing for traffic, so I called to reserve a car and driver and gave a look at my wardrobe to decide on what to wear for my interview. I had packed so lightly for my trip, I found it difficult to be too picky, but I wore the same slightly fitted gray jacket over my black dress. I hadn't had a haircut thus far in my travel, so my slightly wavy hair had grown long and I twisted it and wore it off my neck. All the delicious food and drink I'd consumed hadn't gone to my hips, as yet, so my clothes still fit my 110 pound petite frame. I would have to watch the scales closer as I approached 40, I thought.

In arriving at the location in Edinburgh, I advised the driver I'd give him a ring when it was time to pick me up. Dr. Hammond's assistant asked me to wait while she told him of my arrival. I had arrived right on time, so felt I wouldn't have to wait too long, and in about five minutes he greeted me and apologized for his lateness saying he wanted to seat the panel before bringing me in. We walked down a long hall to a conference room where six other members of the faculty waited.

Later driving back to Aberdeen I had a feeling I had passed muster. The Q&A flowed effortlessly and I had a good feeling about these bright and dedicated educators. I wondered if they offered me the position, and I accepted, would I be acting too hastily without checking other opportunities? Somehow I had confidence that it would be the right decision.

By Friday afternoon, as I began getting ready to see Sam, I had not heard back from Dr. Hammond and I wondered if the news would be negative and how I would handle it. And then the phone rang and Dr. Hammond said, "The position is yours if you want it."

Feeling elated, I showered, put on make-up and pulled my hair up and back and added a silver clip. I put on the gray fitted jacket over my black dress and added a silver beaded short necklace. Adding a dash of Chanel 5, I hastened to answer the door.

Sam stood there for a minute giving me the once over and said, "Wow, lovely lady" and handed me a dozen red roses with the attached poem, Red Red Roses by Burns.

"They're beautiful and meaningful, thank you."

He came in and I excused myself to put the flowers in a vase I found under the sink—apartment manager had thought of everything. I brought the flowers back and placed them on the table which doubled for dining and accent. The main room wasn't very large and opened to the kitchen with stools at a counter. It did have a decent looking dark green and burgundy plaid sofa and overstuffed chair with a lamp on the table between. I put on my all-weather coat, locked up and we took the elevator (lift) to the main floor, where his car awaited.

"No limousine this time?"

"Thought we'd keep it low key."

"This black Mercedes is certainly low key."

"Now you know Lancelot wants to please his lady."

"This lady is pleased with Sir Lancelot."

"Thank you."

We arrived at the restaurant he'd chosen, left the car with the attendant as Sam tucked my arm inside his and we entered a very lovely contemporary space; from a historic architectural granite exterior, to black, red, chrome and glass interior. "Oh, I love it," I gushed.

"I thought you might like something modern for a change."

The hostess greeted him by name and found us a table in an alcove with a window looking out to lights casting their sparkle on the midnight waters. He ordered champagne cocktails for two and starters of ridiculously delicious mixed seafood, including the sweetest of lobster pieces in butter perfect for dipping the chunks of brioche.

"Tell me about your adventures since I saw you last."

"I enjoyed my stay in Dumfries and followed in the footsteps of Burns—his watering holes and farm, and then caught a flight to Aberdeen."

"Did you like the Crathes Castle tour?"

"It was one of the best preserved of the castles I've seen, and supposedly has its resident ghost and magnificent renaissance painted ceilings. It sits on about 500 areas of woodlands and fields and I loved the large walled garden."

"I've read about the ceilings, sorry we couldn't have seen it together, but I've always wanted to visit Castle Fraser, which is the largest Z plan castle in Scotland, would that work for you?"

"Yes, it's on my list."

"I'll pick you up in the morning and we'll spend the day travelling about, if you're game."

"Very much so."

Sam ordered the main (after I told him to surprise me) and since the restaurant specialized in French cuisine, he ordered Chateaubriand for two, medium rare with a sauce balanced perfectly between the tarragon vinegar, shallots, eggs and butter. The absolute best I've ever had, accompanied by a nice red Boudreaux

I managed a comment after the first bite and ready for the second, "I've tried to replicate this sauce a dozen times over the years, and have never achieved anything close to this."

"I think the chef performed some kind of magic."

After dinner we retired to the lounge featuring a live jazz quartet and sipped some cognac.

"If I remember, you can tolerate my jazz obsession."

"Not only tolerate but enjoy. My mother introduced me to jazz at an early age."

The group was made of a sax, piano, trumpet and bass playing mostly soft swing, but doing some up tempo improvising as well. The atmosphere reminded me of jazz clubs I'd visited in San Francisco—dark and understated in order to feature the musicians. Before long both Sam and I had our eyes closed lost in the sounds.

"I hate to say it," he said, "But think we'd better head for home so we'll be bright and bushy tailed in the morning."

"Goodness, I've not heard that expression for some time."

He laughed and said he hadn't either.

We seemed giddy with laughter, partly from our drinks I suspected, as we waited for the attendant to bring the car. "I know you haven't told me all you've been up to, but now we'll have something to visit about tomorrow on our ride through the autumn countryside."

Back at my hotel, he walked me to the door, gave me a light kiss on the cheek, smiled and said goodnight. "I'll pick you up around nine if that's okay with you."

"Please have breakfast with me. I'll give you some freshly ground coffee, scones and fruit."

"Hey, that works for me. Till then goodnight lovely one, and he gave me a hug."

I'm glad he was such a gentleman, I thought, my resistance is very low and I know the time isn't right.

Chapter Sixteen

"**Y**ou make a good cup of coffee."

"Thanks."

After eating our scones and a dish of sliced bananas, pears and strawberries we sat there quietly sipping our second cup of coffee. I somehow couldn't find any words to fill the void.

"You about ready to hit the road?"

"Yes, give me a minute to gather my things."

As I reentered the room, I found Sam sitting on my overstuffed plaid sofa. He looked like he had settled in for a while. I stood looking at him in his jeans and white shirt and solemn good looks and had a catch in my throat.

"Come sit with me Leah."

"I moved slowly to the sofa and sat next to him, still clutching my sweater and purse.

"I know you have something to share with me and why don't we just sit and visit for a while before we head out."

"James is divorcing me," I blurted out.

He looked at me with a stunned look on his face. "Wow that is the last thing I expected to hear."

"He said he has a new friend and they have been sharing our apartment since I left."

"Did he just come right out and tell you that?"

"Yes, and I asked him if he had been seeing her before I left and he said perhaps."

"Perhaps—that's somewhat incriminating."

"I thought so. Anyway, I told him to put my things in the guest bedroom, he could keep the furnishings, and I would send a moving company to pick up my personal items, clothes and car later."

"Is it that easy?"

"Yes, we kept our accounts separate, didn't own any property, nor had children and perhaps that explains the lack of connection we needed. I'm very shocked of James having an affair with one of the PhD candidates, however, and openly living with her, when we both are on the faculty. Middle age crazies I guess."

"Are you going back to settle things?"

"No, I can settle them at a distance. I called my attorney to contact his and send me any papers to sign. I don't want to see James—in my heart perhaps I knew something was amiss when I left and he has been more detached than usual."

I then told Sam about accepting a position at the University of Edinburgh and that I would be starting in January and planned on finding a furnished apartment and could get by until I received my shipment, probably in a couple weeks. He sat there, picked up my hand and held it and said, "You should love working at the University and living in Edinburgh, but you're giving up so much of the work you've done over the years at your own university."

"I know, but I can't go back to where James would be a constant. I'm ready to start over."

"This has to be a shock for you and remember I want to help in any way I can. Instead of visiting a castle today why don't we drive to Edinburgh and I can help you look for an apartment. I know the safest places to live and even know of an apartment community you might like, with water nearby, lots of trails and gardens."

"I will be on a more limited income and have to keep my rent in a moderate range."

"The residents include many teachers from the universities around Edinburg and I think it would be within your budget."

"Are you sure you don't want to see the castle first? We could see it, have lunch and still be in Edinburgh by evening."

"Alright, if you're up to it. The company has an apartment in Edinburgh and we could stay overnight, if that's okay with you, and we would have Sunday to look at more options."

"That sounds good and thanks so much for not just getting up and running away from me. I wouldn't blame you."

"What in the world are you talking about? I'd never want to get up and run away from you. You should know by now how special you are to me. If I'd had my way you'd have left that old James for me a long time ago."

"A long time ago? We've only known each other a few months."

"I knew you were something special on the train ride together in Wales."

He pulled me close and kissed me softly on the lips, then stood up pulled me to my feet and said we needed to get moving. I knew he was right.

As Sam and I drove east on our way to visit the Z shaped castle, I sat quietly looking out to the great expanse of this country I had grown to love. I remembered reading once the land of your ancestors would always be calling for your return. I, of course, thought America to be my land of ancestors for many of them had arrived very early in the New Land. From the great grandfather who arrived on the Mayflower to many arriving in the sixteen hundreds and fighting to survive the bitter winters and in some cases the bitter Native Americans who thought the Pilgrims a threat to their way of life. Of the many encounters with these locals, however, most were peaceful and the new immigrants learned about planting corn and hunting wild turkey and deer, which nourished them and kept them alive during the cold months.

In years to come we destroyed the Native Indian's food source by eliminating great herds of buffalo, we plowed up the native grasses and ruined the soil. We called them savages, broke treaties and put them in reservations. I can't forgive this time in our history.

Aside for its failures, I loved my country; it offered many opportunities to struggling immigrants over the years, and yet at present I find disappointment in how a country, based on immigration, has turned in many ways into a capitalistic economy rather than a democratic state, and is out of balance between rich and poor. I am weary of the constant in-fighting of politician's intent on raising money to stay in office rather than work on issues of state and I especially am disgusted at many of our newscasters and journalists who seemed to reflect the extremes rather than realities—with no attempt at fact finding.

Perhaps being away and not reading the headlines is why I feel comfortable here in Great Britain and especially Scotland, who in so many ways espouses fierce independence along with respect of government. Anyway that is how I see it. And I could also claim it as the land of many ancestors, be them early in history.

About sixteen miles west of Aberdeen we saw the five story tower building looming large in the distance. I had read it was located on 300 acres of woodland and pasture land, and the gray marble structure seemed somehow out of place—like I would expect a red barn, white house, corrals and many animals, instead of the fourteenth century castle standing there like a large gray giant. It was not a ruin, far from it, it had been lovingly restored over the years by the Fraser family and now belonged to the National Trust of Scotland.

We parked and Sam told me the regular summer tours had ended, but he had special permission by the National Trust to visit today. It seemed his company was a donor to the trust.

"I know your company works close to the university system of Great Britain and now it is also involved with the National Trust?"

"We represent education in all its forms and especially for the digital age. My education in computer science, as it involves research and historical preservation, is how I have become head of my department and reek all the benefits. I remain at heart a scientist."

"I'm a professor, but it seems our involvement in digital history coincides."

"Yes, and so many more of our interests. That is our attraction, don't you think?"

"That and how you look in your jeans."

"Back at you."

Castle Fraser is recognized as one of the grandest of baronial tower castles in Scotland. It contains a lovely Great Hall, fine furniture and many of the Fraser portraits. I especially liked the library with the collection of family books. Most impressive is the Wall Garden and many walking paths. Sam and I, holding hands, walked amongst the late fall blossoms and massive trees, by water ponds with sounds of frogs croaking, birds chirping and small wild life scattering off to hide amongst the briar and bushes.

Sam attempted to point out the Z pattern of the castle and I eventually could see how the large tower sat in diagonal to the other towers and formed the Z. In many ways to me it reminded me of a U shape, with the two long halls descending from the towers—but then recognized the angle of the tower that set it off.

"Thanks Sam for your help with these architectural features. I think I have enough notes now to complete a book,"

"Writing was a requirement of your university and your university press would do the publishing. What do you expect from University of Edinburgh?"

"Never hurts to publish and maybe they'll like my book—if not, perhaps I can find someone in the states to publish it."

We drove on to Edinburgh arriving earlier than I thought we would, so we looked around the area Sam thought I'd like to live and he showed me a group of apartments that looked more like individual townhomes, laced with pathways, gardens and ponds. He called the management and made an appointment for in the morning.

"Are you sure this is in my price range?"

"We'll find out tomorrow, but I think you'll be surprised that rents in Scotland are much more reasonable than you're used to."

Sam drove to a luxury hotel, an attendant took the car, and we were escorted to our room by an efficient bell boy, all smiles and warm greeting, as if he had known Sam forever. The executive suite was impressive and after tipping the young man, Sam took my hand and opened the drapes to an expansive view of the inlet waters of the Atlantic Ocean.

"Get comfortable and I'll make us a drink and we'll rest a spell before our dinner reservation here at the hotel."

He showed me to the second bedroom where my suitcase was; thank goodness it was more presentable than my back-pack. I took a quick shower and put on my silk satin loungers and let my now shoulder length hair fall softly. I looked in the mirror and a pair of brown eyes peered back at me; they seemed nervous, or was that my pounding heart. We were alone together again.

"You look lovely, my lovely. I mixed us a couple scotch sours; hope you like it."

I sat down next to him on a black leather and chrome bar stool perched next to a marble topped bar. The drinks were served in a heavy crystal glass. I sipped slowly.

"So good."

"The Scot scotches are too good to resist."

"I agree."

We sat there quietly sipping our drinks, taking glimpses of each other in the large mirror to the back of the bar, lined with about every beverage one could image. Sam had put on some soft music in the background and he finally took my hand and said, "Let's dance."

We glided on the sleek marble floor, swinging in and out of each other's arms, turning and returning and eventually close with my arms around his shoulders and his around my waist.

He lifted me easily in his strong arms, kissed me all the way to his bed. We undressed each other, marveling at every view and touch. Our bodies came together as comfortably as we had come together as companions. It seemed years of yearning went into my coupling with this man; I wanted it to last forever. I was dizzy with emotion.

"It was time sweetheart."

"Oh, thank goodness," I responded, laughing at his serious face looking down at me.

"Give me another chance and I'll last longer next time."

"I'll give you a million more chances, but if we'd gone on any longer I would have passed out from sheer pleasure."

We finally dressed for dinner, both hungry after our exertion. The dining room was as spectacular as the rest of the lovely old hotel and the maître d' greeted Sam and took us to a white linen clothed table with a view of the water.

"Would you like champagne cocktails?" Sam asked.

"Sounds perfect."

We sat there so satisfied with ourselves—I knew I had a glow and Sam seemed to also. Funny how sex with mutual passion can bring so much pleasure. It is as though far from only anticipation, our waiting had brought trust, along with the desire. Or it seemed to me.

We ordered delicately prepared sea bass, bathed in a butter-lemon sauce with dill, fingerling potatoes and baby baked vegetables accompanied by a white French Bordeaux.

"To us, my dear lady."

"To us."

Epilogue

The next day in the autumn of the year Sam and I found me a lovely apartment, within my budget, and we sealed our relationship by spending the rest of the day in bed. As with everything else in our time together our bodies felt as though they had been waiting for each other over our lifetime.

I started my new job in January, amongst a snowy day and sunny faces of my eager learners; bright young students waiting for me to make their time on campus interesting. This was the challenge I looked forward to each year; the opportunity to enhance their interest in history. I had a mixture of students from Scotland, England, Ireland, United States, Australia, Latin American, Mexico, Europe, Asia and the Middle East. Such variety, so new to me, became my absolute favorite year of teaching. It was as if the diversity brought out the best of all of them and me.

Sam came to be with me as many weekends as he could get away and sometimes he could stay the week. We talked about our future together and somehow knew we could fit the pieces together in time. As it was, we enjoyed the time we had, but I did realize I had a ticking clock and we wanted to have some little ones. Soon we thought.

I became pregnant the next year, we married in May and honeymooned in Normandy visiting French chateaux, including that of William the Conqueror known as William, Duke of Normandy, my favorite great grandfather. We still loved our sense of adventure and discovery; architecture to ancestry. I planned on taking a year or two off and we'd live together in London and maybe try for a second little Sam or Samantha.

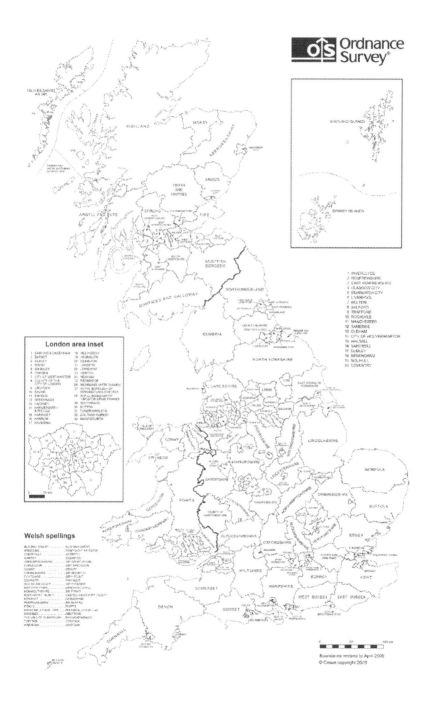

Ordnance
Survey®

London area inset

1 BARKING & DAGENHAM
2 BARNET
3 BEXLEY
4 BRENT
5 BROMLEY
6 CAMDEN
7 CITY OF WESTMINSTER
8 COUNTY OF THE CITY OF LONDON
9 CROYDON
10 EALING
11 ENFIELD
12 GREENWICH
13 HACKNEY
14 HAMMERSMITH & FULHAM
15 HARINGEY
16 HARROW
17 HAVERING
18 HILLINGDON
19 HOUNSLOW
20 ISLINGTON
21 LAMBETH
22 LEWISHAM
23 MERTON
24 NEWHAM
25 REDBRIDGE
26 RICHMOND UPON THAMES
27 ROYAL BOROUGH OF KENSINGTON & CHELSEA
28 ROYAL BOROUGH OF KINGSTON UPON THAMES
29 SOUTHWARK
30 SUTTON
31 TOWER HAMLETS
32 WALTHAM FOREST
33 WANDSWORTH

1 INVERCLYDE
2 RENFREWSHIRE
3 EAST RENFREWSHIRE
4 GLASGOW CITY
5 EDINBURGH CITY
6 LIVERPOOL
7 BOLTON
8 SALFORD
9 TRAFFORD
10 ROCHDALE
11 MANCHESTER
12 TAMESIDE
13 OLDHAM
14 CITY OF WOLVERHAMPTON
15 WALSALL
16 SANDWELL
17 DUDLEY
18 BIRMINGHAM
19 SOLIHULL
20 COVENTRY

Welsh spellings

Boundaries revised to April 2009

© Crown copyright 2009

117